Francis Marion Crawford

A Tale of a Lonely Parish

Vol. I

Francis Marion Crawford

A Tale of a Lonely Parish
Vol. I

ISBN/EAN: 9783337084240

Printed in Europe, USA, Canada, Australia, Japan

Cover: Foto ©Andreas Hilbeck / pixelio.de

More available books at **www.hansebooks.com**

A TALE

OF

A LONELY PARISH

BY

F. MARION CRAWFORD

AUTHOR OF 'MR. ISAACS,' 'DR. CLADIUS,' 'A ROMAN SINGER,'
'ZOROASTER,' ETC.

VOL I.

LONDON

MACMILLAN AND CO.

1886.

TO

My Mother

I DEDICATE THIS TALE

A MEAN TOKEN OF A LIFELONG AFFECTION

SORRENTO, *Christmas Day* 1885.

A TALE OF A LONELY PARISH.

CHAPTER I.

THE Reverend Augustin Ambrose would gladly have given up taking pupils. He was growing old and his sight was beginning to trouble him; he was very weary of Thucydides, of Homer, of the works of Mr. Todhunter of which the green bindings expressed a hope still unrealised, of conic sections—even of his beloved Horace. He was tired of the stupidities of the dull young men who were sent to him because they could not "keep up," and he had long ceased to be surprised or interested by the remarks of the clever ones who were sent to him because their education had not prepared them for an English University. The dull ones could never be made to understand anything, though Mr. Ambrose generally succeeded in making them remember enough to matriculate, by dint of ceaseless repetition and a system of *memoria technica* which embraced most things necessary to the salvation of dull youth. The clever ones, on the other hand, generally lacked altogether the solid foundation of learning; they could construe fluently but did not know a long syllable from a short one; they had vague notions of elemental algebra and no notion at all of arithmetic, but did very well in conic sections; they knew nothing of prosody, but dabbled perpetually in English blank verse; altogether they knew most of those things which they need not have known and they knew none of those things thoroughly which they ought to have known. After twenty years of experience Mr. Ambrose ascertained that it was easier to teach a stupid boy than a clever one, but that he would prefer not to teach at all.

Unfortunately the small tithes of a small country parish in Essex did not furnish a sufficient income for his needs. He had been a Fellow of Trinity College, Cambridge, within a few years of taking his degree, wherein he had obtained high honours.

But he had married and had found himself obliged to accept the first living offered to him, to wit, the vicarage of Billingsfield, whereof his college held the rectory and received the great tithes. The entire income he obtained from his cure never at any time exceeded three hundred and forty-seven pounds, and in the year when it reached that high figure there had been an unusually large number of marriages. It was not surprising that the vicar should desire to improve his circumstances by receiving one or two pupils. He had married young, as has been said, and there had been children born to him, a son and a daughter. Mrs. Ambrose was a good manager and a good mother, and her husband had worked hard. Between them they had brought up their children exceedingly well. The son had in his turn entered the church, had exhibited a faculty of pushing his way which had not characterised his father, had got a curacy in a fashionable Yorkshire watering-place, and was thought to be on the way to obtain a first-rate living. In the course of time, too, the daughter had lost her heart to a young physician who had brilliant prospects and some personal fortune, and the Reverend Augustin Ambrose had given his consent to the union. Nor had he been disappointed. The young physician had risen rapidly in his profession, had been elected a member of the London College, had transferred himself to the capital and now enjoyed a rising practice in Chelsea. So great was his success that it was thought he would before long purchase the goodwill of an old practitioner who dwelt in the neighbourhood of Brompton Crescent, and who, it was said, might shortly be expected to retire.

It will be seen, therefore, that if Mr. Ambrose's life had not been very brilliant, his efforts had on the whole been attended with success. His children were both happy and independent and no longer needed his assistance or support; his wife, the excellent Mrs. Ambrose, enjoyed unfailing health and good spirits; he himself was still vigorous and active, and as yet found no difficulty in obtaining a couple of pupils at two hundred pounds a year each, for he had early got a reputation for successfully preparing young gentlemen with whom no other private tutor could do anything, and he had established the scale of his prices accordingly. It is true that he had sacrificed other things for the sake of imparting tuition, and more than once he had hesitated and asked himself whether he should go on. Indeed, when he graduated, it was thought that he would soon make himself remarkable by the publication of some scholarly work; it was foretold that he might become a famous preacher; it was asserted that he was a general favourite with the Fellows of Trinity and would get a proportionately fat living—but he had committed the unpardonable sin of allowing his chances of fortune to slip from him. He had given up his fellowship, had married and had accepted an insignificant country living. He asked nothing, and he got nothing. He never attracted the notice of his bishop by doing anything extra-ordinary, nor the notice of the public by appearing in print. He baptized, married and buried the people of Billingsfield, Essex, and he took private pupils. He wrote a sermon once a fortnight, and revised old ones for the other three occasions out of four. His sermons were good in their way, but were intended for simple folk and did no justice to the powers he had certainly possessed in his youth. Indeed, as years went on, the dry routine of his life produced its inevitable effect upon his mind, and the productions of Mr. Ambrose grew to be exceedingly commonplace; and the more commonplace he became, the more he regretted having done so little with the faculties he enjoyed, and the more weary he became of the daily task of galvanising the dull minds of his pupils into a spasmodic activity, just sufficient to leap the ditch that separates the schoolboy from the undergraduate. He had not only educated his children and seen them provided for in the world; he had also saved a little money and he had insured his life for five hundred pounds. There was no longer any positive necessity for continuing to teach, as there had been thirty years ago, when he first married.

So much for the circumstances of the Reverend Augustin Ambrose. Personally he was a man of good presence, five feet ten inches in height, active and strong, of a ruddy complexion with smooth, thick gray hair and a plentiful gray beard. He shaved his upper lip however, greatly to the detriment of his appearance, for the said upper lip was very long and the absence of the hirsute appendage showed a very large mouth with very thin lips, generally compressed into an expression of remarkable obstinacy. His nose was both broad and long and his gray eyes were bright and aggressive in their glance. As a matter of fact Mr. Ambrose was combative by nature, but his fighting instincts seem to have been generally employed in the protection of rights he already possessed, rather than in pushing on in search of fresh fields of activity. He was an active man, fond of walking alone and able to walk any distance he pleased; a charitable man with the charity peculiar to people of exceedingly economical tendencies and possessing small fixed incomes. He would give himself vast personal trouble to assist distress, as though aware that since he could not give much money to the poor he was bound to give the best of himself. The good Mrs. Ambrose seconded him in this as in all his works; labouring hard when hard work could do any good, but giving material assistance with a sparing hand. It sufficiently defines the two to say that although many a surly labourer in the parish grumbled that the vicar and his wife were "oncommon near," when money was concerned, there was nevertheless no trouble in which their aid was not invoked and their advice asked. But the indigent labourer not uncommonly retrieved his position by asking a shilling of one of the young gentlemen at the vicarage, who were generally open-handed, good-looking boys, blessed with a great deal more money than brains.

At the time when this tale opens, however, it chanced that one of the two young gentlemen at the vicarage was by no means in the position peculiar to the majority of youths who sought the good offices of the Reverend Augustin Ambrose. John Short, aged eighteen, was in all respects a remarkable contrast to his companion the Honourable Cornelius Angleside. John Short was apparently very poor; the Honourable

Cornelius on the other hand had plenty of money. Short was undeniably clever; Angleside was uncommonly dull. Short was the son of a decayed literary man; Angleside was the son of a nobleman. Short was by nature a hard worker; Angleside was amazingly idle. Short meant to do something in the world; Angleside had early determined to do nothing.

It would not be easy to define the reasons which induced Mr. Ambrose to receive John Short under his roof. He had never before taken a pupil on any but his usual terms, and at his time of life it was strange that he should break through the rule. But here his peculiar views of charity came into play. Short's father had been his own chum at school, and his friend at college, but had failed to reap any substantial benefits from his education. He had been a scholar in his way, but his way had not been the way of other scholars, and when he had gone up for honours he had got a bad third in classics. He would not enter the church, he could not enter the law, he had no interest whatever, and he found himself naturally thrust into the profession of literature. For, a time he had nearly starved ; then he had met with some success and had, of course, married without hesitation ; after this he had had more misfortunes. His wife had died leaving him an only son, whom in course of time he had sent to school. But school was too expensive and he had reluctantly taken the boy home again. It was in a fit of despair that he wrote to his old friend Augustin Ambrose, asking his advice. The Reverend Augustin considered the matter with the assistance of his wife, and being charitable souls, they determined that they must help Short to educate his son. Accordingly the vicar of Billingsfield wrote to his old friend to say that if he could manage to pay a small sum for the lad's board, he, the vicar, would complete the boy's education, so that he might at least have a chance in the world. Short accepted the offer with boundless gratitude and had hitherto not failed to pay the vicar the small sum agreed upon. The result of all this was that Mr. Ambrose had grown very fond of John, and John had derived great advantage from his position. He possessed precisely what his father had lacked, namely a strong bent in one direction, and there was no doubt that he would distinguish himself if he had a chance. That chance the vicar had determined to give him. He had made up his mind that his old friend's son should go to college and show what he was able to do. It was not an easy thing to manage, but the vicar had friends in Cambridge and John had brains; moreover the vicar and John were both very obstinate people and had both determined upon the same plan, so that there was a strong probability of their succeeding.

John Short was eighteen years of age, neither particularly good-looking nor by any means the reverse. He had what bankers commonly call a lucky face; that is to say he had a certain very prepossessing look of honesty in his blue eyes, and a certain look of energetic good will in his features. When he was much older and wore a beard he passed for a handsome man, but at eighteen he could only boast the smallest of fair whiskers, and when anybody took the trouble to look long at him, which was not often, the verdict was

that his jaw was too heavy and his mouth too
obstinate.   In complexion he was fair, and
healthy to look at, generally sunburned in the
summer, for he had a habit of reading out of
doors ; his laugh was very pleasant, though it
was rarely heard ; his eyes were honest but
generally thoughtful ; his frame was sturdy and
already inclined rather to strength than to graceful proportion ; his head matched his body well
being broad and well-shaped with plenty of
prominence over the brows and plenty of fulness
above the temples.   He had a way of standing as
though it would not be easy to move him, and a
way of expressing his opinion which seemed to
challenge contradiction.   But he was not a
combative boy.   If any one argued with him, it
soon appeared that he was not really argument-
ative, but merely enthusiastic.   It was not
necessary to agree with him, and there was small
use in contradicting him.   The more he talked
the more enthusiastic he grew as he developed
his own views ; until seeing that he was not
understood or that he was merely laughed at,
he would end his discourse with a merry laugh

at himself, or a shy apology for having talked so much. But the vicar assured his wife that the boy's Greek and Latin verses were something very extraordinary indeed, and much better than his own in his best days. For John was passionately fond of the classics and did not propose to acquire any more mathematical knowledge than was strictly necessary for his matriculation and " little-go." He meant to be a famous scholar and he meant to get a fellowship at his college in order to be perfectly independent and to help his father.

John was a constant source of wonder to his companion the Honourable Cornelius Angleside, who remembered to have seen fellows of that sort at Eton but had never got near enough to them to know what they were really like. Cornelius had a vague idea that there was some trick about appearing to know so much and that those reading chaps were awful humbugs. How the trick was performed he did not venture to explain, but he was as firmly persuaded that it was managed by some species of conjuring as that Messrs. Maskelyne and Cook performed their wonders by sleight of hand.   That one human brain should actually contain the amount of knowledge John Short appeared to possess was not credible to the Honourable Cornelius, and the latter spent more of his time in trying to discover how John "did it" than in trying to "do it" himself. Nevertheless, young Angleside liked Short after his own fashion, and Short did not dislike Angleside. John's father had given him to understand that as a general rule persons of wealth and good birth were a set of overbearing, purse-proud bullies, who considered men of genius to be little better than a set of learned monkeys, certainly not good enough to black their boots.   For John's father in his misfortunes had imbibed sundry radical notions formerly peculiar to poor literary men, and not yet altogether extinct, and he had accordingly warned his son that all mammon was the mammon of unrighteousness, and that the people who possessed it were the natural enemies of people who had to live by their brains. But John had very soon discovered that though Cornelius Angleside possessed the three qualifica-tions for perdition, in the shape of birth, wealth and ignorance, against which his poor father railed unceasingly, he succeeded nevertheless in making himself very good company. Angleside was not overbearing, he was not purse-proud and he was not a bully. On the contrary he was unobtrusive and sufficiently simple in manner, and he certainly never mentioned the subject of his family or fortune; John rather pitied him, on the whole, until he began to discover that Angleside looked up to him on account of his mental superiority, and then John, being very human, began to like him.

The life at the vicarage of Billingsfield, Essex, was not remarkable for anything but its extreme regularity. Prayers, breakfast, work, lunch, a walk, work, dinner, work, prayers, bed. The programme never varied, save as the seasons introduced some change in the hours of the establishment. The vicar, who was fond of a little gardening and amused himself with a variety of experiments in the laying of asparagus beds, found occasional excitement in the pursuit of a stray cat which had managed to climb his wire netting and get at the heads of his favourite vegetable, in which thrilling chase he was usually aided by an old brown retriever answering, when he answered at all, to the name of Carlo, and by the Honourable Cornelius, whose skill in throwing stones was as phenomenal as his ignorance of Latin quantities. The play was invariably opened by old Reynolds, the ancient and bowlegged gardener, groom and man of all work at the vicarage.

"Please sir, there's Simon Gunn's cat in the sparrer-grass." The information was accompanied by a sort of chuckle of evil satisfaction which at once roused the sleeping passions of the Reverend Augustin Ambrose.

"Dear me, Reynolds, then why don't you turn her out?" and without waiting for an answer, the excellent vicar would spring from his seat and rush down the lawn in the direction of the beds, closely followed by the Honourable Cornelius, who picked up stones from the gravel path as he ran, and whose long legs made short work of the iron fence at the bottom of the garden. Meanwhile the aged Reynolds let Carlo loose from the yard and the hunt was prosecuted with great boldness and ingenuity. The vicar's object was to get the cat out of the asparagus bed as soon as possible without hurting her, for he was a humane man and would not have hurt a fly. Cornelius, on the other hand, desired the game to last as long as possible, and endeavoured to prevent the cat's escape by always hitting the wire netting at the precise spot where she was trying to get over it. In this way he would often succeed in getting as much as half an hour's respite from Horace. At last the vicar, panting with his exertions and bathed in perspiration, would protest against the form of assault.

"Really, Angleside," he would say, "I believe I could throw straighter myself. I'm quite sure Carlo can get her out if you leave him alone."

Whereupon Cornelius would put his hands in his pockets and look on, and in a few minutes, when the cat had been driven out and the vicar's back was turned, he would slip a sixpence into old Reynold's hand, and follow his tutor reluctantly back to the study. Whether there was any connection between the cat and the sixpence is uncertain, but during the last months of

Angleside's stay at the vicarage the ingenuity of Simon Gunn's yellow cat in getting over the wire netting reached such a pitch that the vicar began to prepare a letter to the Bishop Stortford *Chronicle* on the relations generally existing between cats and asparagus beds.

Another event in the life of the vicarage was the periodical lameness of the vicar's strawberry mare, followed by the invariable discovery that George Horsnell the village blacksmith had run a nail into her foot when he shoed her last. Invariably, also, the vicar threatened that in future the mare should be shod by Hawkins the rival blacksmith, who was a dissenter and had consequently never been employed by the vicarage. Moreover it was generally rumoured once every year that old Nat Barker, the octogenarian cripple who had not been able to stand upon his feet for twenty years, was at the point of death. He invariably recovered, however, in time to put in an appearance by proxy at the distribution of a certain dole of a loaf and a shilling on boxing day. It was told also that in remote times the Puckeridge hounds had once come that way and that the fox had got into the churchyard. A repetition of this stirring event was anxiously looked for during many years, every time that the said pack met within ten miles of Billingsfield, but hitherto it had been looked for in vain. On the whole the life at the vicarage was not eventful, and the studies of the two young men who imbibed learning at the feet of the Reverend Augustin Ambrose were rarely interrupted.

Mrs. Ambrose herself represented the feminine element in the society of the little place. The new doctor was a strange man, suspected of being a freethinker, and he was not married. The Hall, for there was a Hall at Billingsfield, was uninhabited, and had been uninhabited for years. The estate which belonged to it was unimportant and moreover was in Chancery and seemed likely to stay there, for reasons no one ever mentioned at Billingsfield, because no one knew anything about them. From time to time a legal looking personage drove up to the Duke's Head, which was kept by Mr. Abraham Boosey, who was also undertaker to the parish, and which was thought to be a very good inn. The legal personage stayed a day or two, spending most of his time at the Hall and in driving about to the scattered farms which represented the estate, but he never came to the vicarage, nor did the vicar ever seem to know what he was doing nor why he came. "He came on business"—that was all that anybody knew. His business was to collect rents, of course; but what he did with them, no one was bold enough to surmise. The estate was in Chancery, it was said, and the definition conveyed about as much to the mind of the average inhabitant of Billingsfield, as if he had been informed that the moon was in perigee or the sun in Scorpio. The practical result of its being in Chancery was that no one lived there.

John Short liked Mrs. Ambrose and the Honourable Cornelius behaved to her with well-bred affability. She always said Cornelius had very nice manners, as indeed he had and had need to have. Occasionally, perhaps four or five times in the year, the Reverend Edward Pewlay, who had what he called a tenor voice, and his wife, who played the pianoforte very fairly, came over to assist at a Penny Reading. He lived "over Harlow way," as the natives expressed it, he was what was called in those parts a rabid Anglican, because he preached in his surplice and had services on the Saints' days, and the vicar of Billingsfield did not sympathise in his views. Nevertheless he was very useful at Penny Readings, and on one of these occasions produced a very ingenious ghost for the delectation of the rustics, by means of a piece of plate glass and a couple of lamps.

There had indeed been festivities at the vicarage to which as many as three clergymen's wives had been invited, but these were rare indeed. For months at a time Mrs. Ambrose reigned in undisputed possession of the woman's social rights in Billingsfield. She was an excellent person in every way. She had once been handsome and even now she was fine-looking, of goodly stature, if also of goodly weight; rosy, even rubicund, in complexion, and rotund of feature; looking at you rather severely out of her large gray eyes, but able to smile very cheerfully and to show an uncommonly good set of teeth; twisting her thick gray hair into a small knot at the back of her head and then covering it with a neatly made cap which she considered becoming to her time of life; dressed always with extreme simplicity and neatness, glorying in her good sense and in her stout shoes; speaking of things which she called "neat" with a devotional admiration and expressing the extremest height of her disapprobation when she said anything was "very untidy." A motherly woman, a practical woman, a good housekeeper and a good wife, careful of small things because generally only small things came in her way, devotedly attached to her husband, whom she regarded with perfect justice as the best man of her acquaintance adding, however, with somewhat precipitous rashness that he was the best man in the world. She took also a great interest in his pupils and busied herself mightily with their welfare. Since the arrival of the new doctor who was suspected of free-thinking, she had shown a strong leaning towards homœopathy, and prescribed small pellets of belladonna for the Honourable Cornelius's cold and infinitesimal drops of aconite for John Short's headaches, until she observed that John never had a headache unless he had worked too much, and Angleside always had a cold when he did not want to work at all. Especially in the department of the commissariat she showed great activity, and the reputation the vicar had acquired for feeding his pupils well had perhaps more to do with his success than he imagined. She was never tired of repeating that Englishmen needed plenty of good food, and she had no principles which she did not practise. She even thought it right to lecture young Angleside upon his idleness at stated intervals. He always replied with great gentleness that he was awfully stupid, you know, and Mr. Ambrose was awfully good about it and he hoped he should not be pulled when he went up. And strange to relate he actually passed his examination and matriculated, to his own immense astonishment and to the no small honour and glory of the Reverend Augustin Ambrose, vicar of Billingsfield, Essex. But when that great day arrived certain events occurred which are worthy to be chronicled and remembered.

CHAPTER II

In the warm June weather young Angleside went
up to pass his examination for entrance at Trinity.
There is nothing particularly interesting or worthy
of note in that simple process, though at that
time the custom of imposing an examination had
only been recently imported from Oxford. For
one whole day forty or fifty young fellows from
all parts of the country sat at the long dining-
tables in the beautiful old hall and wrote as
busily as they could, answering the printed
questions before them, and eyeing each other
curiously from time to time. The weather was
warm and sultry, the trees were all in full leaf
and Cambridge was deserted. Only a few hard-
reading men, who stayed up during the Long,
wandered out with books at the backs of the
colleges or strayed slowly through the empty

courts, objects of considerable interest to the youths who had come up for the entrance examination—chiefly pale men in rather shabby clothes with old gowns and battered caps, and a general appearance of being the worse for wear.

Angleside had been in Cambridge before and consequently lost no time in returning to Billingsfield when the examination was over. Short was to spend the summer at the vicarage, reading hard until the term began, when he was to go up and compete for a minor scholarship; Angleside was to wait until he heard whether he had passed, and was then going abroad to meet his father and to rest from the extreme exertion of mastering the "Apology" and the first books of the "Memorabilia." John drove over to meet the Honourable Cornelius, who was in a terrible state of anxiety and left him no peace on the way asking him again and again to repeat the answers to the questions which had been proposed, reckoning up the ones he had answered wrong and the ones he thought he might have answered right, and coming each time to a different conclusion, finally lighting a huge brierwood pipe and swearing "that it was a beastly shame to subject human beings to such awful torture." John calmed him by saying he fancied Cornelius had "got through"; for John's words were a species of gospel to Cornelius. By the time they reached the vicarage Angleside felt sanguine of his success.

The vicar was not visible. It was a strange and unheard of thing—there were visitors in the drawing-room. This doubtless accounted for the fact that the fly from the Duke's Head was standing on the opposite side of the road. The two young men went into their study, which was on the ground floor and opened upon the passage which led to the drawing-room from the little hall. Angleside remarked that by leaving the door open they would catch a glimpse of the visitor when he went out. But the visitor stayed long. The curiosity of the two was wrought up to a high pitch; it was many months since there had been a real visitor at the vicarage. Angleside suggested going out and finding old Reynolds —he always knew everything that was going on.

"If we only wait long enough," said Short philosophically, "they are sure to come out."

"Perhaps," returned Cornelius rather doubtfully.

"They" did come out. The drawing-room door opened and there was a sound of voices. It was a woman's voice, and a particularly sweet voice, too. Still no one came down the passage. The lady seemed to be lingering in taking her leave. Then there was a sound of small feet and suddenly a little girl stood before the open door of the study, looking wonderingly at the two young men. Short thought he had never seen such a beautiful child. She could not have been more than seven or eight years old, and was not tall for her age; a delicate little figure, all in black, with long brown curls upon her shoulders, flowing abundantly from beneath a round black sailor's hat that was set far back upon her head. The child's face was rather pale than very fair, of a beautiful transparent paleness, with the least tinge of colour in the cheeks; her great violet eyes gazed wonderingly into the study, and her lips parted in childlike uncertainty, while her little gloved hand rested on the door-post as though to get a sense of security from something so solid.

It was only for a moment. Both the young fellows smiled at the child unconsciously. Perhaps she thought they were laughing at her; she turned and ran away again; then passed a second time, stealing a long glance at the two strangers, but followed immediately by the lady, who was probably her mother, and whose voice had been heard for the last few moments. The lady, too, glanced in as she went by, and John Short lost his heart then and there; not that the lady was beautiful as the little girl was, but because there was something in her face, in her figure, in her whole carriage, that moved the boy suddenly as she looked at him and sent the blood rushing to his cheeks and forehead.

She seemed young, but he never thought of her age. In reality she was nine-and-twenty years old but looked younger. She was pale, far paler than the little girl, but she had those same violet eyes, large, deep and sorrowful, beneath dark, smooth eyebrows that arched high and rose a little in the middle. Her mouth was perhaps large for her face but her full lips curved gently and seemed able to smile, though she was not smiling. Her nose was perhaps too small—her face was far from faultless—and it had the slightest tendency to turn up instead of down, but it was so delicately modelled that an artist would have pardoned it that deviation from the classic. Thick brown hair waved across her white forehead and was hidden under the black bonnet and the veil thrown back over it. She was dressed in black and the close-fitting gown showed off with unconscious vanity the lines of a perfectly moulded and perfectly supple figure. But it was especially her eyes which attracted John's sudden attention at that first glance, her violet eyes, tender, sad, almost pathetic, seeming to ask sympathy and marvellously able to command it.

It was but for a moment that she paused. Then came the vicar, following her from the drawing-room, and all three went on. Presently Short heard the front door open and Mr Ambrose shouted to the fly.

"Muggins! Muggins!"

No one had ever been able to say why Abraham Boosey, the publican, had christened his henchman with an appellation so vulgar, to say the least of it——so amazingly cacophonous. The man's real name was plain Charles Bird; but Abraham Boosey had christened him Muggins and Muggins he remained. Muggins had had some beer and was asleep, for the afternoon was hot and he had anticipated his "fours."

Short saw his opportunity and darted out of the study to the hall where the lady and her little girl were waiting while the vicar tried to rouse the driver of the fly by shouting at him. John blushed again as he passed close to the woman with the sad eyes; he could not tell why, but the blood mounted to the very roots of his hair, and for a moment he felt very foolish.

"I'll wake him up, Mr. Ambrose," he said, running out hatless into the summer's sun.

"Wake up, you lazy beggar!" he shouted in the ear of the sleeping Muggins, shaking him violently by the arm as he stood upon the wheel. Muggins grunted something and smiled rather idiotically. "It was only the young gentleman's play," he would have said. Bless you! he did not mind being shaken and screamed at! He slowly turned his horses and brought the fly up to the door. John walked back and stood waiting.

"Thank you," said the lady in a voice that made his heart jump, as she came out from under the porch and the vicar helped her to get in. Then it was the turn of the little girl.

"Good-bye, my dear," said the vicar kindly as he took her hand.

"Good-bye," said the child. Then she hesitated and looked at John, who was standing beside the clergyman. "Good-bye," she repeated, holding out her little hand shyly towards him. John took it and grew redder than ever as he felt that the lady was watching him. Then the little girl blushed and laughed in her small embarrassment, and climbed into the carriage.

"You will write, then?" asked Mr. Ambrose as he shut the door.

"Yes—and thank you again. You are very, very kind to me," answered the lady, and John thought that as she spoke there were tears in her voice. She seemed very unhappy and to John she seemed very beautiful. Muggins cracked his whip and the fly moved off, leaving the vicar and his pupil standing together at the iron wicket gate before the house.

"Well? Do you think Angleside got through?" asked Mr. Ambrose, rather anxiously.

Short said he thought Angleside was safe. He hoped the vicar would say something about the lady, but to his annoyance, he said nothing at all. John could not ask questions, seeing it was none of his business and was fain to content himself with thinking of the lady's face and voice. He felt very uncomfortable at dinner. He thought the excellent Mrs. Ambrose eyed him with unusual severity, as though suspecting what he was thinking about, and he thought the vicar's gray eye twinkled occasionally with the pleasant sense of possessing a secret he had no intention of imparting. As a matter of fact Mrs. Ambrose was supremely unconscious of the fact that John had seen the lady, and looked at him with some curiosity, observing that he seemed nervous and blushed from time to time and was more silent than usual. She came to the conclusion that he had been working too hard, as usual, and that night requested him to take two little pellets of aconite, and to repeat the dose in the morning. Whether it was the result of the homœopathic medicine or of the lapse of a few hours and a good night's rest, it is impossible to say; John, however, was himself again the next morning and showed no further signs of nervousness. But he kept his eyes and ears open, hoping for some news of the exquisite creature who had made so profound an impression on his heart.

In due time the joyful news arrived from Cambridge that the Honourable Cornelius had passed his examination and was at liberty to matriculate at the beginning of the term. The intelligence was duly telegraphed to his father, and in a few hours came a despatch in answer, full of affectionate congratulation and requesting that Cornelius should proceed at once to Paris, where his father was waiting for him. The young man took an affectionate leave of the vicar, of Mrs. Ambrose and especially of John Short, for whom he had conceived an almost superstitious admiration; old Reynolds was not forgotten in the farewell, and for several days after Angleside's departure the aged gardener was observed to walk somewhat unsteadily and to wear a peculiarly thoughtful expression; while the vicar observed with annoyance that Strawberry, the old mare, was less carefully groomed than usual. Strangely coincident with these phenomena was the fact that Simon Gunn's yellow cat seemed to have entirely repented of her evil practices, renouncing from the day when Cornelius left for Paris her periodical invasion of the asparagus beds at the foot of the garden. But the vicar was too practical a man to waste time in speculating upon the occult relations of seemingly disconnected facts. He applied himself with diligence to the work of preparing John Short to compete for the minor scholarship. The labour was congenial. He had never taken a pupil so far before, and it was a genuine delight to him to bring his own real powers into play at last. As the summer wore

on, he predicted all manner of success for John
Short, and his predictions were destined before
long to be realised, for John did all he promised
to do and more also. To have succeeded in
pushing the Honourable Cornelius through his
entrance examination was a triumph indeed, but
an uninteresting one at best, and one which had
no further consequences. But to be the means
of turning out the senior classic of the University
was an honour which would not only greatly
increase the good vicar's reputation but would
be to him a source of the keenest satisfaction
during the remainder of his life ; moreover
the prospects which would be immediately opened
to John in case he obtained such a brilliant
success would be a very material benefit to his
unlucky father, whose talents yielded him but
a precarious livelihood and whose pitiable condition had induced his old schoolfellow to under-
take the education of his son.

Much depended upon John's obtaining one or
more scholarships during his career at college.
To a man of inferior talents the vicar would
have suggested that it would be wiser to go to

a smaller college than Trinity where he would have less competition to expect; but as soon as he realised John's powers, he made up his mind that it would be precisely where competition was hottest that his pupil would have the greatest success. He would get something— perhaps his father would make a little more money—the vicar even dreamed of lending John a small sum—something would turn up; at all events he must go to the largest college and do everything in the best possible way. Meanwhile he must work as hard as he could during the few months remaining before the beginning of his first term.

Whether the lady ever wrote to Mr. Ambrose, John could not ascertain; she was never mentioned at the vicarage, and it seemed as though the mystery were never to be solved. But the impression she had made upon the young man's mind remained and even gained strength by the working of his imagination; for he thought of her night and day, treasuring up every memory of her that he could recall, building romances in his mind, conceiving the most ingenious reasons for the solitary visit she had made to the vicarage, and inwardly vowing that if ever he should be at liberty to follow his own inclinations he would go out into the world and search for her. He was only eighteen then, and of a strongly susceptible temperament. He had seen nothing of the world, for even when living in London, in a dingy lodging, with his father, he had been perpetually occupied with books, reading much and seeing little. Then he had been at school, but he had seen the dark side of school life—the side which boys who are known to be very poor generally see; and more than ever he had resorted to study for comfort and relief from outward ills. Then at last he had been transferred to a serener state in the vicarage of Billingsfield and had grown up rapidly from a schoolboy to a young man; but, as has been said, the feminine element at the vicarage was solely represented by Mrs. Ambrose and the monotony of her maternal society was varied only by the occasional visits of the mild young Mrs. Edward Pewlay. John Short had indeed a powerful and aspiring imagination, but it would have been impossible even by straining that faculty to its utmost activity to think in the same breath of romance and of Mrs. Ambrose, for even in her youth Mrs. Ambrose had not been precisely a romantic character. John's fancy was not stimulated by his surroundings, but it fed upon itself and grew fast enough to acquire an influence over everything he did. It was not surprising that, when at last chance threw in his way a being who seemed instantly to realise and fulfil his wildest dreams of beauty and feminine fascination, he should have yielded without a struggle to the delicious influence, feeling that henceforth his ideal had taken shape and substance, and had thereby become more than ever the ideal in which he delighted.

He gave her names, a dozen of them every day, christening her after every heroine in fiction and history of whom he had ever read. But no name seemed to suit her well enough; whereupon he wrote a Greek ode and a Latin epistle to the fair unknown, but omitted to show them to the Reverend Augustin Ambrose, though he was quite certain that they were the best he had ever produced. Then he began to write a novel, but suddenly recollected that a famous author had written one entitled " No Name," and as that was the only title he could possibly give to the work he contemplated he of course had no choice but to abandon the work itself. He wrote more verses, and he dreamed more dreams, and he meanwhile acquired much learning and in process of time realised that he had but a few days longer to stay at Billingsfield. The Michaelmas term was about to open and he must bid farewell to the hospitable roof and the learned conversation of the good vicar. But when those last days came he realised that he was leaving the scene of his only dream, and his heart grew sad.

Indeed he loved the old red brick vicarage with its low porch, overgrown with creepers, its fragrant old flower garden, surrounding it on three sides, its gabled roof, its south wall whereon the vicar constantly attempted to train fig trees, maintaining that the climate of England had grown warmer and that he would prove it— John loved it all, and especially he loved the little study, lined with the books grown familiar to him, and the study door, the door through which he had seen that lovely face which he firmly believed was to inspire him to do great things and to influence his whole life for ever after. He would leave the door open and place himself just where he had sat that day, and then he would look suddenly up with beating heart, almost fancying he could again see those violet eyes gazing at him from the dusky passage— blushing then to himself, like any girl, and burying himself in his book till the fancy was grown too strong and he looked up again. He had attempted to sketch her face on a bit of paper; but he had no skill and he thrust the drawing into the paper basket, horrified at having made anything so hideous in the effort to represent anything so beautiful, and returned to making odes upon her, and Latin epistles, in which he succeeded much better.

And now the time had come when he must leave all this dreaming, or at least the scene of it, and go to college and win scholarships and renown. It was hard to go and he showed his regret so plainly that Mrs. Ambrose was touched at what she took for his affection for the place and for herself and for the vicar. John Short was indeed very grateful to her for all the kindness she had shown him, and to Mr. Ambrose for the learning he had acquired; for John was a fine fellow and never forgot an obligation nor undervalued one. But when we are very young our hearts are far more easily touched to joy and sadness by the chords and discords of our own dreaming, than by the material doings of the world around us, or by the strong and benevolent interest our elders are good enough to take in us. We feel grateful to those same elders if we have any good in us, but we are far from feeling a similar interest in them. We see in our imaginations wonderful pictures, and we hear wonderful words, for everything we dream of partakes of an unknown perfection and completely throws into the shade the inartistic commonplaces of daily life. As John Short grew older, he often regretted the society of his old tutor and in the frequent absence of important buttons from his raiment he bitterly realised that there was no longer a motherly Mrs. Ambrose to inspect his linen; but when he took leave of them what hurt him most was to turn his back upon the beloved old study, upon the very door through which he had once, and only once, beheld the ideal of his first love dream.

Though the vicar was glad to see the boy started upon what he already regarded as a career of certain victory, he was sorry to lose him, not knowing when he should see him again. John intended to read through all the vacations until he got his degree. He might indeed have come down for a day or two at Christmas, but with his very slender resources even so short a pleasure trip was not to be thought of lightly. It was therefore to be a long separation, so long to look forward to that when John saw the shabby little box which contained all his worldly goods put up into the back of the vicar's dogcart, and stood at last in the hall, saying good-bye, he felt as though he was being thrust out into the world never to return again, his heart seemed to rise in his throat, the tears stood in his eyes and he could hardly speak a word. Even then he thought of that day when he had waked up the sleepy Muggins to take away the beautiful unknown lady. He felt he must be quick about his leave-taking, or he would break down.

"You have been very good to me. I—I shall never forget it," he murmured as he shook hands with Mrs. Ambrose. "And you, too, sir—" he added turning to the vicar. But the old clergyman cut him short, being himself rather uncertain about the throat.

"Good-bye, my lad. God bless you. We shall hear of you soon—showing them what you can do with your Alcaics—Good-bye."

So John got into the dogcart and was driven off by the ancient Reynolds—past the "Duke's Head," past the "Feathers," past the churchyard and the croft—the "croat," they called it in Billingsfield—and on by the windmill on the heath, a hideous bit of grassless common euphemistically so named, and so out to the high-road towards the railway station, feeling very miserable indeed. It is a curious fact, too, in the history of his psychology that in proportion as he got farther from the vicarage he thought more and more of his old tutor and less and less of his unfinished dream, and he realised painfully that the vicar was nearly the only friend he had in the world. He would of course find Cornelius Angleside at Cambridge, but he suspected that Cornelius, turned loose among a merry band of undergraduates of his own position would be a very different person from the idle youth he had known at Billingsfield, trembling in the intervals of his idleness at the awful prospect of the entrance examination, and frantically attempting to master some bit of stray knowledge which might possibly be useful to him. Cornelius would hunt, would gamble, would go to the races and would give wines at college; John was to be a reading man who must avoid such things as he would avoid the devil himself, not only because he was too wretchedly poor to have any share whatever in the amusements of Cornelius and his set, but because every minute was important, every hour meant not only learning but meant, most emphatically, money. He thought of his poor father, grinding out the life of a literary hack in a wretched London lodging, dining Heaven knew where and generally supping not at all, saving every penny to help his son's education, hard working, honest, lacking no virtue except the virtue of all virtues—success. Then he thought how he himself had been favoured by fortune during these last years, living under the vicar's roof, treated with the same consideration as the high-born young gentlemen who had been his companions, living well, sleeping well and getting the best education in England for nothing or next to nothing, while that same father of his had never ceased to slave day and night with his pen, honestly doing his best and yet enjoying none of the good things of life. John thought of all this and set his teeth boldly to face the world. A few months, he thought, and he might have earned a scholarship—he might be independent. Then a little longer—less than three years and he might, nay, he would, take high honours in the university and come back crowned with glory, with the prospect of a fellowship, with every profession open to him, with the world at his feet and with money in his hand to help his father out of all his troubles.

That was how John Short went to Trinity. It was a hard struggle at first, for he found himself much poorer than he had imagined, and it seemed as though the ends could not possibly meet. There was no question of denying himself luxuries; that would have been easy enough. In those first months it was the necessities that he lacked, the coals for his little grate, the oil for his one small lamp. But he fought bravely through it, having, like many another young fellow who has weathered the storms of poverty in pursuit of learning, an iron constitution, and an even stronger will. He used to say long afterwards that feeling cold was a mere habit and that when one thoroughly understood the construction of Greek verses, some stimulus of physical discomfort was necessary to make the imagination work well; in support of which assertion he said that he had never done such good things by the comfortable fire in the study at Billingsfield vicarage as he did afterwards on winter nights by the light of a tallow candle, high up in Neville's Court. Moreover, if any one argued that it was better for an extremely poor man not to go to Trinity, but to some much smaller college, he answered that as far as he himself was concerned he could not have done better, which was quite true and therefore perfectly unanswerable. Where the competition was less, he would have been satisfied with less, he said; where it was greatest a man could only be contented when he had reached the highest point possible. But before he attained his end he suffered more than any one knew, especially during those first months. For when he had got his first scholarship, he insisted upon sending back the little sums of hard-earned money his father sent him from time to time, and he consequently had nearly as hard work as before to keep himself warm and to keep oil in his lamp during the long winter's evenings. But he succeeded, nevertheless.

CHAPTER III.

In the month of October of that year, a short time after John had taken up his abode in Trinity College, an event occurred which shook Billingsfield to its foundations; no less an event than the occupation of the dwelling known as the "cottage." What the cottage was will appear hereafter. The arrival of the new tenants occurred in the following manner.

The Reverend Augustin Ambrose received a letter, which he immediately showed to his wife, as he showed most of his correspondence; for he was of the disposition which may be termed wife-consulting. Married men are generally of two kinds; those who tell their wives everything and those who tell them nothing. It is evident that the relative merits of the two systems depend chiefly upon the relative merits of the wives in question. Mr. Ambrose had no doubt of the advantages of his own method and he carried it to its furthest expression, for he never did anything whatever without consulting his better half.   On the whole the plan worked well, for the vicar had learning and his wife had common sense. He therefore showed the letter to her and she read it, and read it again, and finally put it away, writing across the envelope in her own large, clear hand the words—Goddard, Cottage—indicative of the contents.

" My Dear Sir—It is now nearly five months since I saw you last. Need I tell you that the sense of your kindness is still fresh in my memory? You do not know, indeed you cannot know, what an impression your goodness made upon me. You showed me that I was acting rightly. It has been so hard to act rightly. Of course you quite understand what I mean. I cannot refer to the great sorrow which has overtaken me and my dear innocent little Nellie. There is no use in referring to it, for I have told you all. You allowed me to unburden my heart to you during my brief visit, and ever since that day I have felt very much, I may say infinitely, relieved.

"I am again about to ask you a favour; I trust indeed that I am not asking too much, but I know by experience how kind you are and so I am not afraid to ask this too. Do you remember speaking to me of the little cottage? The picture you drew of it quite charmed me, and I have determined to take it, that is, if it is still to be let and if it is not asking quite too much of you. I mean, if you will take it for me. You cannot think how grateful I shall be and I enclose a cheque. I am almost sure you said thirty-six pounds. It was thirty-six, was it not? The reason I venture to enclose the money is because you are so very kind, but of course you do not know anything certain about me. But I am sure you will understand. You said you were sure I could live with my little girl in Billingsfield for three hundred a year. I find I have a little more, in fact nearly five hundred. If you tell me that I can have the cottage, I will come down at once, for town is very dreary and we have been here all summer except a week at Margate. Let me thank you again, you have been so very kind, and believe me, my dear sir, very sincerely yours,

"MARY GODDARD."

"Augustin, my dear, this is very exciting," said Mrs. Ambrose, as she handed the cheque to her husband for inspection and returned the letter to its envelope, preparatory to marking it for future reference; and when, as has been said, she had written upon the outside the words —Goddard, Cottage, and had put it away she turned upon her husband with an inquiring manner peculiar to her. Mr. Ambrose was standing before the window, looking out at the rain and occasionally glancing at the cheque he still held in his hand.

"Just like a woman to send a cheque to 'bearer' through the post," he remarked, severely. "However since I have got it, it is all right."

"I don't think it is all right, Augustin," said his wife. "We are taking a great responsibility in bringing her into the parish. I am quite sure she is a dissenter or a Romanist or something dreadful, to begin with."

"My dear," answered the vicar, mildly, "you make very uncharitable suppositions. It seems to me that the most one can say of her is that she is very unhappy and that she does not write very good English."

"Oh, I have no doubt she is very unhappy. But as you say we must not be uncharitable. I suppose you will have to write about the cottage."

"I suppose so," said Mr. Ambrose doubtfully. "I cannot send her back the money, and the cottage is certainly to let."

He deposited the cheque in the drawer of his writing-table and began to walk up and down the room, glancing up from time to time at his wife who was lifting one after another the ornaments which stood upon the chimney-piece, in order to ascertain whether Susan had dusted underneath them. She had many ways of assuring herself that people did their work properly.

"No," said she, " you cannot send her back

the money. But it is a very solemn responsibility. I hope we are doing quite right."

"I certainly would not hesitate to return the cheque, my dear, if I thought any harm would come of Mrs. Goddard's living here. But I don't think there is any reason to doubt her story."

"Of course not. It was in the *Standard,* so there is no doubt about it. I only hope no one else reads the papers here."

"They read them in the kitchen," added Mrs. Ambrose presently, "and they probably take a paper at the Duke's Head. Mr. Boosey is rather a literary character."

"Nobody will suppose it was that Goddard, my dear," said the vicar in a reassuring tone of voice.

"No—you had better write about the cottage."

"I will," said the vicar; and he forthwith did. And moreover, with his usual willingness to give himself trouble for other people, he took a vast deal of pains to see that the cottage was really habitable. It turned out to be in very good condition. It was a pretty place enough, standing ten yards back from the road, beyond the village, just opposite the gates of the park; a little square house of red brick with a high pointed roof and a little garden. The walls were overgrown with creepers which had once been trained with considerable care, but which during the last two years had thriven in un-trimmed luxuriance and now covered the whole of the side of the house which faced the road. So thickly did they grow that it was with difficulty that the windows could at first be opened. The vicar sighed as he entered the darkened rooms. His daughter had lived in the cottage when she first married the young doctor who had now gone to London, and the vicar had been, and was, very fond of his daughter. He had almost despaired of ever seeing her again in Billingsfield; the only glimpses of her he could obtain were got by going himself to town, for the doctor was so busy that he always put off the projected visit to the country and his wife was so fond of him that she refused to go alone. The vicar sighed as he forced open the windows upon the lower floor and let the light into the bare and empty rooms which had once been so bright and full of happiness. He wondered what sort of person Mrs. Goddard would turn out to be upon nearer acquaintance, and made vague, unconscious conjectures about her furniture as he stumbled up the dark stairs to the upper story.

He was not left long in doubt. The arrangements were easily concluded, for the cottage belonged to the estate in Chancery and the lawyer in charge was very busy with other matters. The guarantee afforded by the vicar's personal application, together with the payment of a year's rent in advance so far facilitated matters that four days after she had written to Mr. Ambrose the latter informed Mrs. Goddard that she was at liberty to take possession. The vicar suggested that the Billingsfield carrier, who drove his cart to London once a week, could bring her furniture down in two trips and save her a considerable expense; Mrs. Goddard accepted this advice and in the course of a fortnight was installed with all her goods in the cottage. Having completed her arrangements at last, she came to call upon the vicar's wife.

Mrs. Goddard had not changed since she had first visited Billingsfield, five months earlier, though little Eleanor had grown taller and was if possible prettier than ever. Something of the character of the lady in black may have been gathered from the style of her letter to Mr Ambrose; that communication had impressed the vicar's wife unfavourably and had drawn from her husband a somewhat compassionate remark about the bad English it contained. Nevertheless when Mrs. Goddard came to live in Billingsfield the Ambroses soon discovered that she was a very well-educated woman, that she appeared to have read much and to have read intelligently, and that she was on the whole decidedly interesting. It was long, however, before Mrs. Ambrose entirely conquered a certain antipathy she felt for her, and which she explained after her own fashion. Mrs. Goddard was not a dissenter and she was not a Romanist; on the contrary she appeared to be a very good churchwoman. She paid her bills regularly and never gave anybody any trouble. She visited the vicarage at stated intervals, and the vicarage graciously returned her visits.   The vicar himself even went to the cottage more often than Mrs. Ambrose thought strictly necessary, for the vicar was strongly prejudiced in her favour.   But Mrs. Ambrose did not share that prejudice.   Mrs. Goddard, she said, was too effusive, talked too much about herself and her troubles, did not look thoroughly straightforward, probably had foreign blood.   Ay, there was the rub—Mrs. Ambrose suspected that Mrs. Goddard was not quite English.   If she was not, why did she not say so, and be done with it?

Mrs. Goddard was English, nevertheless, and would have been very much surprised could she have guessed the secret cause of the slight coldness she sometimes observed in the manner of the clergyman's wife towards her.   She herself, poor thing, believed it was because she was in trouble, and considering the nature of the disaster which had befallen her, she was not surprised.   She was rather a weak woman, rather timid, and if she talked a little too much sometimes it was because she felt embarrassed; there were times, too, when she was very silent and sad.   She had been very happy and the great catastrophe had overtaken her suddenly, leaving her absolutely without friends. She wanted to be hidden from the world, and by one of those strange contrasts often found in weak people she had suddenly made a very bold resolution and had successfully carried it out. She had come straight to a man she had never seen, but whom she knew very well by reputation, and had told him her story and asked him to help her; and she had not come in vain. The person who advised her to go to the Reverend Augustin Ambrose knew that there was not a better man to whom she could apply. She had found what she wanted, a sort of deserted village where she would never be obliged to meet any one, since there was absolutely no society; she had found a good man upon whom she felt she could rely in case of further difficulty; and she had not come upon false pretences, for she had told her whole story quite frankly. For a woman who was naturally timid she had done a thing requiring considerable courage, and she was astonished at her own boldness after she had done it. But in her peaceful retreat, she reflected that she could not possibly have left England, as many women in her position would have done, simply because the idea of exile was intolerable to her; she reflected also that if she had settled in any place where there was any sort of society her story would one day have become known, and that if she had spent years in studying her situation she could not have done better than in going boldly to the vicar of Billingsfield and explaining her sad position to him. She had found a haven of rest after many months of terrible anxiety and she hoped that she might end her days in peace and in the spot she had chosen. But she was very young—not thirty years of age yet—and her little girl would soon grow up—and then? Evidently her dream of peace was likely to be of limited duration; but she resigned herself to the unpleasant possibilities of the future with a good grace, in consideration of the advantages she enjoyed in the present.

Mrs. Ambrose was at home when Mrs. Goddard and little Eleanor came to the vicarage. Indeed

Mrs. Ambrose was rarely out in the afternoon, unless something very unusual called her away. She received her visitor with the stern hospitality she exercised towards strangers. The strangers she saw were generally the near relations of the young gentlemen whom her husband received for educational purposes. She stood in the front drawing-room, that is to say, in the most impressive chamber of that fortress which is an Englishman's house. It was a formal room, arranged by a fixed rule and the order of it was maintained inflexibly; no event could be imagined of such terrible power as to have caused the displacement of one of those chairs, of one of those ornaments upon the chimney-piece, of one of those engravings upon the walls. The walls were papered with one shade of green, the furniture was covered with material of another shade of green and the well-spared carpet exhibited still a third variety of the same colour. Mrs. Ambrose's sense of order did not extend to the simplest forms of artistic harmony, but when it had an opportunity of impressing itself upon inanimate objects which were liable to

be moved, washed or dusted, its effects were
formidable indeed.   She worshipped neatness
and cleanliness; she left the question of taste
to others.   And now she stood in the keep of
her stronghold, the impersonation of moral recti-
tude and of practical housekeeping.

Mrs. Goddard entered rather timidly, followed
by little Eleanor whose ideas had been so much
disturbed by the recent change in her existence,
that she had grown unusually silent and her
great violet eyes were unceasingly opened wide
to take in the growing wonders of her situation.
Mrs. Goddard was still dressed in black, as when
John Short had seen her five months earlier.
There was something a little peculiar in her
mourning, though Mrs. Ambrose would have
found it hard to, define the peculiarity.   Some
people would have said that if she was really
a widow her gown fitted a little too well, her
bonnet was a little too small, her veil a little
too short.   Mrs. Ambrose supposed that those
points were suggested by the latest fashions
in London and summed up the difficulty by
surmising that Mrs. Goddard had foreign blood.

"I should have called before," said the latter, deeply impressed by the severe appearance of the vicar's wife, "but I have been so busy putting my things into the cottage——"

"Pray don't think of it," answered Mrs. Ambrose. Then she added after a pause, "I am very glad to see you." She appeared to have been weighing in her conscience the question whether she could truthfully say so or not. But Mrs. Goddard was grateful for the smallest advances.

"Thank you," she said, "you are so very kind. Will you tell Mr. Ambrose how thankful I am for his kind assistance? Yes, Nellie and I have had hard work in moving, have not we, dear?" She drew the beautiful child close to her and gazed lovingly into her eyes. But Nellie was shy; she hid her face on her mother's shoulder, and then looked doubtfully at Mrs. Ambrose, and then hid herself again.

"How old is your little girl?" asked Mrs. Ambrose more kindly. She was fond of children, and actually pitied any child whose mother perhaps had foreign blood.

"Eleanor—I call her Nellie—is eight years

old. She will be nine in January. She is tall for her age," added Mrs. Goddard with affectionate pride. As a matter of fact Nellie was small for her years, and Mrs. Ambrose, who was the most truthful of women, felt that she could not conscientiously agree in calling her tall. She changed the subject.

"I am afraid you will find it very quiet in Billingsfield," she said presently.

"Oh, I am used—that is, I prefer a very quiet place. I want to live very quietly for some years, indeed I hope for the rest of my life. Besides it will be so good for Nellie to live in the country—she will grow so strong."

"She looks very well, I am sure," answered Mrs. Ambrose rather bluntly, looking at the child's clear complexion and bright eyes. "And have you always lived in town until now, Mrs. Goddard?" she asked.

"Oh no, not always, but most of the year, perhaps. Indeed I think so." Mrs. Goddard felt nervous before the searching glance of the elder woman. Mrs. Ambrose concluded that she was not absolutely straightforward.

"Do you think you can make the cottage comfortable?" asked the vicar's wife, seeing that the conversation languished.

"Oh, I think so," answered her visitor, glad to change the subject, and suddenly becoming very voluble as she had previously been very shy. "It is really a charming little place. Of course it is not very large, but as we have not got very many belongings that is all the better; and the garden is small but extremely pretty and wild, and the kitchen is very convenient; really I quite wonder how the people who built it could have made it all so comfortable. You see there are one—two—the pantry, the kitchen and two rooms on the ground floor and plenty of room upstairs for everybody, and as for the sun! it streams into all the windows at once from morning till night. And such a pretty view, too, of that old gate opposite—where does it lead to, Mrs. Ambrose? It is so very pretty."

"It leads to the park and the Hall," answered Mrs. Ambrose.

"Oh—" Mrs. Goddard's tone changed. "But nobody lives there?" she asked suddenly.

"Oh no—it is in Chancery, you know."

"What—what is that, exactly?" asked Mrs. Goddard, timidly. "Is there a young heir waiting to grow up—I mean waiting to take possession?"

"No. There is a suit about it. It has been going on for forty years my husband says, and they cannot decide to whom it belongs."

"I see," answered Mrs. Goddard. "I suppose they will never decide now."

"Probably not for some time."

"It must be a very pretty place. Can one go in, do you think? I am so fond of trees— what a beautiful garden you have yourself, Mrs. Ambrose."

"Would you like to see it?" asked the vicar's wife, anxious to bring the visit to a conclusion.

"Oh, thank you—of all things!" exclaimed Mrs. Goddard. "Would not you like to run about the garden, Nellie?"

The little girl nodded slowly and stared at Mrs. Ambrose.

"My husband is a very good gardener," said the latter, leading the way out to the hall. "And so was John Short, but he has left us, you know."

"Who was John Short?" asked Mrs. Goddard rather absently, as she watched Mrs. Ambrose who was wrapping herself in a huge blue waterproof cloak and tying a sort of worsted hood over her head.

" He was one of the boys Mr. Ambrose prepared for college—such a good fellow.   You may have seen him when you came last June, Mrs. Goddard?"

" Had he very bright blue eyes—a nice face?"

" Yes—that is, it might have been Mr. Angleside —Lord Scatterbeigh's son—he was here, too."

" Oh," said Mrs. Goddard, " perhaps it was."

" Mamma," asked little Nellie, " what is Laws Catterbay ?"

" A peer, darling."

" Like the one at Brighton, mamma, with a band ?"

" No, child," answered the mother laughing. " P, double E, R, peer—a rich gentleman."

" Like poor papa then ?" inquired the irrepressible Eleanor.

Mrs. Goddard turned pale and pressed the little girl close to her side, leaning down to whisper in her ear.

"You must not ask foolish questions, darling
—I will tell you by and by."

"Papa was a rich gentleman," objected the
child.

Mrs. Goddard looked at Mrs. Ambrose, and the
ready tears came into her eyes. The vicar's wife
smiled kindly and took little Nellie by the hand.

"Come, dear," she said in the motherly tone
that was natural to her when she was not receiving
visitors. "Come and see the garden and you
can play with Carlo."

"Can't I see Laws Catterbay, too?" asked the
little girl rather wistfully.

"Carlo is a great, big, brown dog," said Mrs.
Ambrose, leading the child out into the garden,
while Mrs. Goddard followed close behind. Before
they had gone far they came upon the vicar,
arrayed in an old coat, his hands thrust into a
pair of gigantic gardening gloves and a battered
old felt hat upon his head. Mrs. Goddard had felt
rather uncomfortable in the impressive society
of Mrs. Ambrose and the sight of the vicar's
genial face was reassuring in the extreme. She
was not disappointed, for he immediately relieved

the situation by asking all manner of kindly questions, interspersed with remarks upon his garden, while Mrs. Ambrose introduced little Nellie to the acquaintance of Carlo who had not seen so pretty a little girl for many a day, and capered and wagged his feathery tail in a manner most unseemly for so clerical a dog.

So it came about that Mrs. Goddard established herself at Billingsfield and made her first visit to the vicarage. After that the ice was broken and things went on smoothly enough. Mrs. Ambrose's hints concerning foreign blood, and her husband's invariable remonstrance to the effect that she ought to be more charitable, grew more and more rare as time went on, and finally ceased altogether. Mrs. Goddard became a regular institution, and ceased to astonish the inhabitants. Mr. Thomas Reid, the sexton, was heard to remark from time to time that he " didn't hold with th'm newfangle fashins in dress;" but he was a regular old conservative, and most people agreed with Mr. Abraham Boosey of the Duke's Head, who had often been to London, and who said she did "look just A one, slap up, she did !"

Mrs. Goddard became an institution, and in the course of the first year of her residence in the cottage it came to be expected that she should dine at the vicarage at least once a week; and once a week, also, Mr. and Mrs. Ambrose went up and had tea with her and little Eleanor at the cottage. It came to pass also that Mrs. Goddard heard a vast deal of talk about John Short and his successes at Trinity, and she actually developed a lively interest in his career, and asked for news of him almost as eagerly as though he had been already a friend of her own. In very quiet places people easily get into the sympathetic habit of regarding their neighbours' interests as very closely allied to their own. The constant talk about John Short, the vicar's sanguine hopes for his brilliant future, and Mrs. Ambrose's unlimited praise of his moral qualities, repeated day by day and week by week produced a vivid impression on Mrs. Goddard's mind. It would have surprised her and even amused her beyond measure had she had any idea that she herself had for a long time absorbed the interest of this same John Short, that he had written hundreds of Greek and Latin verses in her praise, while wholly ignorant of her name, and that at the very time when without knowing him, she was constantly mentioning him as though she knew him intimately well, he himself was looking back to the one glimpse he had had of her, as to a dream of unspeakable bliss.

It never occurred to Mr. Ambrose's mind to tell John in the occasional letters he wrote that Mrs. Goddard had settled in Billingsfield. John, he thought, could take no possible interest in knowing about her, and moreover, Mrs. Goddard herself was most anxious never to be mentioned abroad. She had come to Billingsfield to live in complete obscurity, and the good vicar had promised that as far as he and his wife were concerned she should have her wish. To tell even John Short, his own beloved pupil, would be to some extent a breach of faith, and there was assuredly no earthly reason why John should be told. It might do harm, for of course the young fellow had made acquaintances at Cambridge; he had probably read about the Goddard case in the papers, and might talk about it. If he should happen to come down for a day or two he would probably meet her; but that could not be avoided. It was not likely that he would come for some time. The vicar himself intended to go up to Cambridge for a day or two after Christmas to see him; but the winter flew by and Mr. Ambrose did not go. Then came Easter, then the summer and the Long vacation. John wrote that he could not leave his books for a day, but that he hoped to run down next Christmas. Again he did not come, but there came the news of his having won another and a more important scholarship; the news also that he was already regarded as the most promising man in the university, all of which exceedingly delighted the heart of the Reverend Augustin Ambrose, and being told with eulogistic comments to Mrs. Goddard, tended to increase the interest she felt in the existence of John Short, so that she began to long for a sight of him, without exactly knowing why.

Gradually, too, as she and her little girl passed many peaceful days in the quiet cottage, the sad woman's face grew less sorrowful. She spoke of herself more cheerfully and dwelt less upon the subject of her grief. She had at first been so miserable that she could hardly talk at all without referring to her unhappy situation though, after her first interview with Mrs. Ambrose, no one had ever heard her mention any details connected with her trouble. But now she never approached the subject at all. Her face lost none of its pathetic beauty, it is true, but it seemed to express sorrow past rather than present. Meanwhile little Nellie grew daily more lovely, and absorbed more and more of her mother's attention.

CHAPTER IV.

EVENTS of such stirring interest as the establishment of Mrs. Goddard in Billingsfield rarely come alone; for it seems to be in the nature of great changes to bring other changes with them, even when there is no apparent connection whatever between them. It took nearly two years for Billingsfield to recover from its astonishment at Mrs. Goddard's arrival, and before the excitement had completely worn off the village was again taken off its feet by unexpected news of stupendous import, even as of old Pompeii was overthrown by a second earthquake before it had wholly recovered from the devastation caused by the first. The shock was indeed a severe one. The Juxon estate was reported to be out of Chancery, and a new squire was coming to take up his residence at the Hall.

It is not known exactly how the thing first

became known, but there was soon no doubt whatever that it was true. Thomas Reid, the sexton, who remembered that the old squire died forty years ago come Michaelmas, and had been buried in a "wonderful heavy" coffin, Thomas Reid the stern censor of the vicar's sermons, a melancholic and sober man, so far lost his head over the news as to ask Mr. Ambrose's leave to ring the bells, Mr. Abraham Boosey having promised beer for the ringers. Even to the vicar's enlightened mind it seemed fitting that there should be some festivity over so great an event and the bells were accordingly rung during one whole afternoon. Thomas Reid's ringers never got beyond the first "bob" of a peal, for with the exception of the sexton himself and old William Speller the wheelwright, who pulled the treble bell, they were chiefly dull youths who with infinite difficulty had been taught what changes they knew by rote and had very little idea of ringing by scientific rule. Moreover Mr. Boosey was liberal in the matter of beer that day and the effect of each successive can that was taken up the stairs of the old tower was immediately apparent to every one within hearing, that is to say as far as five miles around.

The estate was out of Chancery at last. For forty years, ever since the death of the old squire, no one had rightfully called the Hall his own. The heir had lived abroad, and had lived in such an exceedingly eccentric manner as to give ground for a suit *de lunatico inquirendo*, brought by another heir. With the consistency of judicial purpose which characterises such proceedings the courts appeared to have decided that though the natural possessor, the eccentric individual who lived abroad, was too mad to be left in actual possession, he was not mad enough to justify actual possession in the person of the next of kin. Proceedings continued, fees were paid, a certain legal personage already mentioned came down from time to time and looked over the estate, but the matter was not finally settled until the eccentric individual died, after forty years of eccentricity, to the infinite relief and satisfaction of all parties and especially of his lawful successor Charles James Juxon now, at last, " of Billingsfield Hall, in the county of Essex, Esquire."

In due time also Mr. Juxon appeared. It was natural that he should come to see the vicar, and as it happened that he called late in the afternoon upon the day when Mrs. Goddard and little Eleanor were accustomed to dine at the vicarage, he at once had an opportunity of making the acquaintance of his tenant; thus, if we except the free-thinking doctor, it will be seen that Mr. Juxon was in the course of five minutes introduced to the whole of the Billingsfield society.

He was a man inclining towards middle age, of an active and vigorous body, of a moderate intelligence and of decidedly prepossessing appearance. His features were of the strong square type, common to men whose fathers for many generations have lived in the country. His eyes were small, blue and very bright, and to judge from the lines in his sunburned face he was a man who laughed often and heartily. He had an abundance of short brown hair, parted very far upon one side and brushed to a phenomenal smoothness, and he wore a full brown beard, cut rather short and carefully trimmed, He immediately won the heart of Mrs. Ambrose on account of his extremely neat appearance. There was no foreign blood in him, she was sure. He had large clean hands with large and polished nails. He wore very well made clothes, and he spoke like a gentleman. The vicar, too, was at once prepossessed in his favour, and even little Eleanor, who was generally very shy before strangers, looked at him admiringly and showed little of her usual bashfulness. But Mrs. Goddard seemed ill at ease and tried to keep out of the conversation as much as possible.

"There have been great rejoicings at the prospect of your arrival," said the vicar when the new-comer had been introduced to both the ladies. "I fancy that if you had let it be known that you were coming down to-day the people would have turned out to meet you at the station."

"The truth is, I rather avoid that sort of thing," said the squire, smiling. "I would rather enter upon my dominions as quietly as possible."

"It is much better for the people, too," remarked Mrs. Ambrose. "Their idea of a holiday is to do no work and have too much beer."

"I daresay that would not hurt them much," answered Mr. Juxon cheerfully. "By the bye, I know nothing about them. I have never been here before. My man of business wanted to come down and show me over the estate, and introduce me to the farmers and all that, but I thought it would be such a bore that I would not have him."

"There is not much to tell, really," said Mr. Ambrose. "The society of Billingsfield is all here," he added with a smile, "including one of your tenants."

"Are you my tenant?" asked Mr. Juxon pleasantly, and he looked at Mrs. Goddard.

"Yes," said she, "I have taken the cottage."

"The cottage? Excuse me, but you know I am a stranger here—what is the cottage?"

"Such a pretty place," answered Mrs. Ambrose, "just opposite the park gate. You must have seen it as you came down."

"Oh, is that it?" said the squire. "Yes, I saw it, and I wished I lived there instead of in the Hall. It looks so comfortable and small. The Hall is a perfect wilderness."

Mrs. Goddard felt a sudden fear lest her new landlord should take it into his head to give her notice. She only took the cottage by the year and her present lease ended in October. The arrival of a squire in possession at the Hall was a catastrophe to which she had not looked forward. The idea troubled her. She had accidentally made Mr. Juxon's acquaintance, and she knew enough of the world to understand that in such a place he would regard her as a valuable addition to the society of the vicar and the vicar's wife. She would meet him constantly; there would be visitors at the Hall—she would have to meet them, too. Her dream of solitude was at an end. For a moment she seemed so nervous that Mr. Juxon observed her embarrassment and supposed it was due to his remark about living in the cottage himself.

"Do not be afraid, Mrs. Goddard," he said quickly, "I am not going to do anything so uncivil as to ask you to give up the cottage.

Besides, it would be too small, you know."

"Have you any family, Mr. Juxon?" inquired

Mrs. Ambrose with a severity which startled the squire. Mrs. Ambrose thought that if there was a Mrs. Juxon, she had been unpardonably deceived. Of course Mr. Juxon should have said that he was married as soon as he entered the room.

"I have a very large family," answered the squire, and after enjoying for a moment the surprise he saw in Mrs. Ambrose's face, he added with a laugh, "I have a library of ten thousand volumes—a very large family indeed. Otherwise I have no encumbrances, thank heaven."

"You are a scholar?" asked Mr. Ambrose eagerly.

"A book fancier, only a book fancier," returned the squire modestly. "But I am very fond of the fancy."

"What is a book fancier, mamma?" asked little Eleanor in a whisper. But Mr. Juxon heard the child's question.

"If your mamma will bring you up to the Hall one of these days, Miss Goddard, I will show you. A book fancier is a terrible fellow who has lots of books, and is pursued by a large evil genius telling him he must buy every book he sees, and that he will never by any possibility read half of them before he dies."

Little Eleanor stared for a moment with her great violet eyes, and then turning again to her mother, whispered in her ear.

"Mamma, he called me Miss Goddard!"

"Run out and play in the garden, darling," said her mother with a smile. But the child would not go and sat down on a stool and stared at the squire, who was immensely delighted.

"So you are going to bring all your library, Mr. Juxon?" asked the vicar returning to the charge.

"Yes—and I beg you will make any use of it you please," answered the visitor. "I have a great fondness for books and I think I have some valuable volumes. But I am no great scholar, as you are, though I read a great deal. I have always noticed that the men who accumulate great libraries do not know much, and the men who know a great deal have very few books. Now I will wager that you have not a thousand volumes in your house, Mr. Ambrose."

"Five hundred would be nearer the mark," said the vicar.

"The fewer one has the nearer one approaches to Aquinas's *homo unius libri,*" returned the squire. "You are nine thousand five hundred degrees nearer to ideal wisdom than I am."

Mr. Ambrose laughed.

"Nevertheless," he said, "You may be sure that if you give me leave to use your books, I will take advantage of the permission. It is in writing sermons that one feels the want of a good library."

"I should think it would be an awful bore to write sermons," remarked the squire with such perfect innocence that both the vicar and Mrs. Goddard laughed loudly. But Mrs. Ambrose eyed Mr. Juxon with renewed severity.

"I should fancy it would be a much greater bore, as you call it, to the congregation if my husband never wrote any new ones," she said stiffly. Whereat the squire looked rather puzzled, and coloured a little. But Mr. Ambrose came to the rescue.

"Yes, indeed, my wife is quite right. There are no people with such terrible memories as churchwardens. They remember a sermon twenty years old. But as you say, the writing of sermons is not an easy task when a man has been at it for thirty years and more. A man begins by being enthusiastic, then his mind gets into a groove and for some time, if he happens to like the groove, he writes very well. But by and by he has written all there is to be said in the particular line he has chosen and he does not know how to choose another. That is the time when a man needs a library to help him."

"I really don't think you have reached that point, Mr. Ambrose," remarked Mrs. Goddard. She admired the vicar and liked his sermons.

"You are fortunately not in the position of my churchwardens," answered Mr. Ambrose. "You have not been listening to me for thirty years."

"How long have you been my tenant, Mrs. Goddard?" asked the squire.

"Nearly two years," she answered thoughtfully, and her sad eyes rested a moment upon Mr. Juxon's face with an expression he remembered. Indeed he looked at her very often and as he looked his admiration increased, so that when he rose to take his leave the predominant impression of the vicarage which remained in his mind was that of her face. Something of the same fascination took hold of him which had seized upon John Short when he caught sight of Mrs. Goddard through the open door of the study, something of that unexpected interest which in Mrs. Ambrose had at first aroused a half suspicious dislike, now long forgotten.

Before the squire left he invited the whole party to come and dine with him at the Hall on the following Saturday. He must have some kind of a house-warming, he said, for he was altogether too lonely up there. Mrs. Goddard would bring Eleanor, of course; they would dine early—it would not be late for the little girl. If they all liked they could call it tea instead of dinner. Of course everything was topsy-turvy in the Hall, but they would excuse that. He hoped to establish friendly relations with his vicar and with his tenant — his fair tenant. Might he call soon and see whether there was any thing that could be done to improve the cottage? Before the day when they were all coming to dine? He would call to-morrow, then. Anything that needed doing should be done, Mrs. Goddard might be sure. When the books arrived he would let Mr. Ambrose know, of course, and they would have a day together.

So he went away, leaving the impression that he was a very good-natured and agreeable man. Even Mrs. Ambrose was mollified. He had shocked her by his remark about sermon writing, but he had of course not meant it, and he appeared to mean to be very civil. It was curious to see how all severity vanished from Mrs. Ambrose's manner so soon as the stranger who aroused it was out of sight and hearing. She appeared as a formidably stern type of the British matron to the chance visitors who came to the vicarage; but they were no sooner gone than her natural temper was restored and she was kindness and geniality itself.

But Mrs. Goddard was very thoughtful. She was not pleased at the fact of an addition to the Billingsfield community, and yet she liked the appearance of the squire. He had declared his intention of calling upon her on the following day, and she would be bound to receive him. She was young, she had been shut off from the world for two years, and the prospect of Mr. Juxon's acquaintance was in itself not unpleasant; but the idea that he was to be permanently established in the Hall frightened her. She had felt since she came to Billingsfield that from the very first she had put herself upon a footing of safety by telling her story to the vicar. But the vicar would not without her permission repeat that story to Mr. Juxon. Was she herself called upon to do so? She was a very sensitive woman, and her impressionable nature had been strongly affected by what she had suffered. An almost morbid fear of seeming to make false pretences possessed her. She was more than thirty years of age, it is true, but she saw plainly enough in her glass that she was more than passably good-looking still. There were one or two gray threads in her brown waving hair and she took no trouble to remove them; no one ever noticed them. There were one or two lines, very faint lines, in her forehead; no one ever saw them. She could hardly see them herself. Supposing—why should she not suppose it?—supposing Mr. Juxon were to take a fancy to her, as a lone bachelor of forty and odd might easily take a fancy to a pretty woman who was his tenant and lived at his gate, what should she do?   He was an honest man, and she was a conscientious woman; she could not deceive him, if it came to that.   She would have to tell him the whole truth.   As she thought of it, she turned pale and trembled.   And yet she had liked his face, she had told him he might call at the cottage, and her woman's instinct foresaw that she was to see him often.   It was not vanity which made her think that the squire might grow to like her too much.   She had had experiences in her life and she knew that she was attractive; the very fear she had felt for the last two years lest she should be thrown into the society of men who might be attracted by her, increased her apprehension tenfold.   She could not look forward with indifference to the expected visit, for the novelty of seeing any one besides the vicar and his wife was too great; she could not refuse to see the squire, for he would come again and again until she received him; and yet, she could not get rid of the idea that there was danger in seeing him. Call it as one may, that woman's instinct of peril is rarely at fault.

In the late twilight of the June evening Mrs. Goddard and Eleanor walked home together by the broad road which led towards the park gate.

"Don't you think Mr. Juxon is very kind, mamma?" asked the child.

"Yes, darling, I have no doubt he is. It was very good of him to ask you to go to the Hall."

"And he called me Miss Goddard," said Eleanor. "I wonder whether he will always call me Miss Goddard."

"He did not know your name was Nellie," explained her mother.

"Oh, I wish nobody knew, mamma. It was so nice. When shall I be grown up, mamma?"

"Soon, my child—too soon," said Mrs. Goddard with a sigh. Nellie looked at her mother and was silent for a minute.

"Mamma, do you like Mr. Juxon?" she asked presently.

"No, dear—how can one like anybody one has only seen once?"

"Oh—but I thought you might," said Nellie. ' Don't you think you will, mamma? Say you will—do!"

"Why?" asked her mother in some surprise. "I cannot say anything about it. I daresay he is very nice."

"It will be so delightful to go to the Hall to dinner and be waited on by big real servants— not like Susan at the vicarage, or Martha. Won't you like it, mamma? Of course Mr. Juxon will have real servants, just like—like poor papa." Nellie finished her speech rather doubtfully as though not sure how her mother would take it. Mrs. Goddard sighed again, but said nothing. She could not stop the child's talking—why should Nellie not speak of her father? Nellie did not know.

"I think it will be perfectly delightful," said Nellie, seeing she got no answer from her mother, and as though putting the final seal of affirmation to her remarks about the Hall. But she appeared to be satisfied at not having been contradicted and did not return to the subject that evening.

Mr. Juxon lost no time in keeping his word and on the following morning at about eleven o'clock, when Mrs. Goddard was just hearing the last of Nellie's lesson in geography and little Nellie herself was beginning to be terribly tired of acquiring knowledge in such very warm weather, the squire's square figure was seen to emerge from the park gate opposite, clad in gray knickerbockers and dark green stockings, a rose in his buttonhole and a thick stick in his hand, presenting all the traditional appearance of a thriving country gentleman of the period. He crossed the road, stopped a moment and whistled his dog to heel and then opened the wicket gate that led to the cottage. Nellie sprang to the window in wild excitement.

"Oh what a dog!" she cried. "Mamma, *do* come and see! And Mr. Juxon is coming, too —he has green stockings!"

But Mrs. Goddard, who was not prepared for so early a visit, hastily put away what might be described as the débris of Nellie's lessons, to wit, a much thumbed book of geography, a well worn spelling book, a very particularly inky piece of blotting paper, a pen of which most the of stock had been subjected to the continuous action of Nellie's teeth for several months, and an ancient doll, without the assistance of which, as a species of Stokesite *memoria technica*, Nellie declared that she could not say her lessons at all. Those things disappeared, and, with them, Nellie's troubles, into a large drawer set apart for the purpose. By the time Mr. Juxon had rung the bell and Martha's answering footstep was beginning to echo in the small passage, Mrs. Goddard had passed to the consideration of Nellie herself. Nellie's fingers were mightily inky, but in other respects she was presentable.

"Run and wash your hands, child, and then you may come back," said her mother.

"Oh mamma, *must* I go? He's just coming in." She gave one despairing look at her little hands, and then ran away. The idea of missing one moment of Mr. Juxon's visit was bitter, but to be caught with inky fingers by a beautiful gentleman with green stockings and a rose in his coat would be more terribly humiliating still.

There was a sound as of some gigantic beast plunging into the passage as the front door was opened, and a scream of terror from Martha followed by a good-natured laugh from the squire.

"You'll excuse *me*, sir, but he don't bite, sir, does he?   Oh my! what a dog he is, sir——"

"Is Mrs. Goddard in?" inquired Mr. Juxon, holding the hound by the collar.   Martha opened the door of the little sitting-room and the squire looked in.   Martha fled down the passage.

"Oh my!   What a tremendious dog that is, to be sure!" she was heard to exclaim as she disappeared into the back of the cottage.

"May I come in?" asked Mr. Juxon, rather timidly and with an expression of amused perplexity on his brown face.   "Lie down, Stamboul!"

"Oh, bring him in, too," said Mrs. Goddard coming forward and taking Mr. Juxon's hand. "I am so fond of dogs."   Indeed she was rather embarrassed and was glad of the diversion.

"He is really very quiet," said the squire apologetically, "only he is a little impetuous about getting into a house."   Then, seeing that Mrs. Goddard looked at the enormous animal with some interest and much wonder, he added, " he is a Russian bloodhound—perhaps you never saw one? He was given to me in Constantinople, so I call him Stamboul—good name for a big dog is not it ?"

"Very," said Mrs. Goddard rather nervously. Stamboul was indeed an exceedingly remarkable beast. Taller than the tallest mastiff, he combined with his gigantic strength and size a grace and swiftness of motion which no mastiff can possess. His smooth clean coat, of a perfectly even slate colour throughout, was without folds, close as a greyhound's, showing every articulation and every swelling muscle of his body. His broad square head and monstrous jaw betrayed more of the quickness and sudden ferocity of the tiger than those suggested by the heavy, lion-like jowl of the English mastiff. His ears, too, were close cropped, in accordance with the Russian fashion, and somehow the compactness this gave to his head seemed to throw forward and bring into prominence his great fiery eyes, that reflected red lights as he moved, and did not tend to inspire confidence in the timid stranger.

"Do sit down," said Mrs. Goddard, and when the squire was seated Stamboul sat himself down upon his haunches beside him, and looked slowly from his master to the lady and back again, his tongue hanging out as though anxious to hear what they might have to say to each other.

"I thought I should be sure to find you in the morning," began Mr. Juxon, after a pause. "I hope I have not disturbed you?"

"Oh, not at all. Nellie has just finished her lessons."

"The fact is," continued the squire, "that I was going to survey the nakedness of the land which has fallen to my lot, and as I came out of the park I saw the cottage right before me and I could not resist the temptation of calling. I had no idea we were such near neighbours."

"Yes," said Mrs. Goddard, "it is very near."

Mr. Juxon glanced round the room. He was not exactly at a loss for words, but Mrs. Goddard did not seem inclined to encourage the conversation. He saw that the room was not only exceedingly comfortable but that its arrangement betrayed a considerable taste for luxury. The furniture was of a kind not generally seen in cottages, and appeared to have formed part of some ·great establishment. The carpet itself was of a finer and softer kind than any at the Hall. The writing-table was a piece of richly inlaid work, and the implements upon it were of the solid, severe and valuable kind that are seen in rich men's houses. A clock which was undoubtedly of the Louis Quinze period stood upon the chimney-piece. On the walls were hung three or four pictures which, Mr. Juxon thought, must be both old and of great value. Upon a little table by the fireplace lay four or five objects of Chinese jade and Japanese ivory and a silver chatelaine of old workmanship. The squire saw, and wondered why such a very pretty woman, who possessed such very pretty things, should choose to come and live in his cottage in the parish of Billingsfield. And having seen and wondered he became interested in his charming tenant and endeavoured to carry on the conversation in a more confidential strain.

CHAPTER V.

"You have done more towards beautifying the cottage than I could have hoped to do," said Mr. Juxon, leaning back in his chair and resting one hand on Stamboul's great head.

"It was very pretty of itself," answered Mrs. Goddard, "and fortunately it is not very big, or my things would look lost in it."

"I should not say that—you have so many beautiful things. They seem to suit the place so well. I am sure you will never think of taking them away."

"Not if I can help it—I am too glad to be quiet."

"You have travelled a great deal, Mrs. Goddard?" asked the squire.

"No—not exactly that—only a little, after all. I have not been to Constantinople for instance," she added looking at the hound Mr. Juxon had brought from the East. "You are indeed a traveller."

"I have travelled all my life," said the squire, indifferently, as though the subject of his wanderings did not interest him. "From what little I have seen of Billingsfield I fancy you will find all the quiet you could wish, here. Really, I realise that at my own gate I must come to you for information. What sort of man is that excellent rector down there, whom I met last night?"

The squire's tone became more confidential as he put the question.

"Well—he is not a rector, to begin with," answered Mrs. Goddard with a smile, "he is the vicar, and he is a most good man, whom I have always found most kind."

"I can readily fancy that," said Mr. Juxon. "But his wife seems to be of the severe type."

"No—she struck me so at first, too. · I think it is only with strangers. She is such a motherly sort of woman, you do not know ! She only has that little manner when you first meet her."

"What a strange thing that is!" remarked the squire, looking at Mrs. Goddard. "The natural belief of English people in each other's depravity until they have had time to make acquaintance! And is there no one else here—no doctor—no doctor's wife?"

"Not a soul," answered Mrs. Goddard. "There is a doctor, but the vicarage suspects him of free thought. He certainly never goes to church. He has no wife."

"This is the most Arcadian retreat I ever was in. Upon my word, I am a very lucky man."

"I suppose that it must be a relief when one has travelled so much," replied Mrs. Goddard.

"Or suffered very much," added the squire, half unconsciously, looking at her sad face.

"Yes," she answered. At that moment the door opened and Nellie entered the room, having successfully grappled with the inkstains. She went straight to the squire, and held out her hand, blushing a little, but looking very pretty. Then she saw the huge head of Stamboul who looked up at her with a ferociously agreeable canine smile, and thwacked the carpet with his tail as he sat; Nellie started back.

"Oh, what a dog!" she exclaimed. But very soon she was on excellent terms with him; little Nellie was not timid, and Stamboul, who liked people who were not afraid of him and was especially fond of children, did his best to be amusing.

"He is a very good dog," remarked Mr. Juxon. "He once did me a very good service."

"How was that?"

"I was riding in the Belgrade forest one summer. I was alone with Stamboul following. A couple of ruffians tried to rob me. Stamboul caught one of them."

"Did he hurt him very much?"

"I don't know—he killed him before the fellow could scream, and I shot the other," replied the squire calmly.

"What a horrible story!" exclaimed Mrs. Goddard, turning pale. "Come here, Nellie—don't touch that dreadful dog!"

"Do not be afraid—he is perfectly harmless. Come here Stamboul!" The huge beast obeyed, wagging his tail, and sat down at his master's feet, still looking rather wistfully at Nellie who had been playing with him. "You see," continued Mr. Juxon, "he is as quiet as a lamb— would not hurt a fly!"

"I think it is dreadful to have such animals about," said Mrs. Goddard in a low voice, still looking at the dog with horror.

"I am sorry I told you. It may prejudice you against him. I only meant to explain how faithful he is, that is all. You see a man grows fond of a creature that has saved his life."

"I suppose so, but it is rather startling to see such an animal so near to one. I fear I am very nervous."

"By the bye," said the squire with the bold irrelevancy of a man who wants to turn the subject, "are you fond of flowers?"

"I?" said Mrs. Goddard in surprise. "Yes— very. Why?"

"I thought you would not mind if I had the garden here improved a little. One might put in a couple of frames. I did not see any flowers about.   I am so fond of them myself, you see, that I always look for them."

"You are very kind," answered Mrs. Goddard. "But I would not have you take any trouble on my account.   We are so comfortable and so fond of the cottage already——"

"Well, I hope you will grow to like it even better," returned the squire with a genial smile. "Anything I can do, you know—" he rose as though to take his leave.   "Excuse me, but may I look at that picture?   Andrea del Sarto? Yes, I thought so—wonderful—upon my word, in a cottage in Billingsfield.   Where did you find it?"

"It was my husband's," said Mrs. Goddard.

"Ah—ah, yes," said the squire in a subdued tone.   "I beg your pardon," he added, as people often do, unconsciously, when they fancy they have accidentally roused in another a painful train of thought.   Then he turned to go.   "We dine at half-past seven, you know, so as to be early for Miss Nellie," he said, as he went out.

Mrs. Goddard was glad he was gone, though she felt that he was not unsympathetic.   The story of the dog had frightened her, and her own mention of her husband had made her nervous and sad. More than ever she felt that fear of being in a false position, which had assailed her when she had first met the squire on the previous evening. He had at once opened relations with her in a way which showed that he intended to be intimate; he had offered to improve her cottage, had insisted upon making frames in her garden, had asked her to dinner with the Ambroses and had established the right to talk to her whenever he got a chance. He interested her, too, which was worse. His passing references to his travels and to his adventures, of which he spoke with the indifference of a man accustomed to danger, his unassuming manner, his frank ways —everything about him awakened her interest. She had supposed that in two years the very faculty of being interested by a man would be dulled if not destroyed; she found to her annoyance that though she had seen Mr. Juxon only twice she could not put him out of her thoughts. She was, moreover, a nervous, almost morbid, woman, and the natural result of trying to forget his existence was that she could think of nothing else.

How much better it would be, she thought, if he knew her story from the first. He might then be as friendly as he pleased; there would be no danger in it, to him or to her. She almost determined to go at once and ask the vicar's advice. But by the time she had nearly made up her mind it was the hour for luncheon, and little Nellie's appetite was exigent. By the time lunch was over her determination had changed. She had reflected that the vicar would think her morbid, that, with his usual good sense, he would say there was no necessity for telling the squire anything; indeed, that to do so would be undignified. If the squire were indeed going to lead the life of a recluse as he proposed doing, he was not really a man to cause her any apprehension. If he had travelled about the world for forty years without having his heart disturbed by any of the women he must have met in that time, he was certainly not the kind of man, when once he had determined to settle in his home, to fall in love with the first pretty woman he met.

It was absurd; there was no likelihood of it; it was her own miserable vanity, she told herself, which made the thing seem probable, and she would not think any more about it. She, a woman thirty-one years of age, with a daughter who ere long would be growing up to womanhood! To be afraid of a mere stranger like Mr. Juxon—afraid lest he should fall in love with her! Could anything be more ridiculous? Her duty was to live quietly as she had lived before, to take no more notice of the squire than was necessary in order to be civil, and so all would be well.

And so it seemed for a long time. The squire improved the garden of the cottage and Mrs. Goddard and Nellie, with the Ambroses, dined at the Hall, which at first seemed an exceedingly dreary and dismal place, but which, as they returned thither again and again, grew more and more luxurious, till the transformation was complete. Mr. Juxon brought all manner of things to the house; vans upon vans arrived, laden with boxes of books and pictures and oriental carpets and rare objects which the squire had collected in

his many years of travel, and which he appeared
to have stored in London until he had at last
inherited the Hall.   The longer the Ambroses
and Mrs. Goddard knew him, the more singularly
impressed they were with his reticence concerning
himself.   He appeared to have been everywhere,
to have seen everything, and he had certainly
brought back a vast collection of more or less
valuable objects from his travels, besides the
large library he had accumulated and which
contained many rare and curious editions of
ancient books.   He was evidently a man of very
good education, and a much better scholar than
he was willing to allow.   The vicar delighted in
his society and when the two found themselves
together in the great room which Mr. Juxon had
lined with well-filled shelves, they remained for
hours absorbed in literary and scholastic talk.
But whenever the vicar approached the subject of
the squire's past life, the latter became vague
and gave ambiguous answers to any direct questions addressed to him.   He evidently disliked
talking of himself, though he would talk about
anything else that occurred to him with a fluency

which Mrs. Ambrose declared was the only un-English thing about him. The consequence was that the vicar became more and more interested in his new acquaintance, and though the squire was so frank and honest a man that it was impossible to suspect him of any doubtful action in the past, Mr. Ambrose suspected that he had a secret. Indeed after hearing the story Mrs. Goddard had confided to his ears, nothing would have surprised the vicar. After finding that so good, so upright and so honourable a woman as the fair tenant of the cottage could be put into such a singularly painful position as that in which she now found herself, it was not hard to imagine that this singular person who had inherited the Hall might also have some weighty reason for loving the solitude of Billingsfield.

To chronicle the small events which occurred in that Arcadian parish, would be to overstep the bounds of permissible tediousness. In such places all events move slowly and take long to develop to their results. The passions which in our own quickly moving world spring up, flourish, wither and are cut down in a month require when they are not stimulated by the fertilising heat of artificial surroundings, a longer period for their growth; and when that growth is attained they are likely to be stronger and more deeply rooted. It is not true that the study of them is less interesting, nor that they have less importance in themselves. The difficulty of narrative is greater when they are to be described, for it is necessary to carry the imagination in a short time over a long period, to show how from small incidents great results follow, and to show also how the very limited and trivial nature of the surroundings may cause important things to be overlooked. Amidst such influences acquaintance is soon made between the few persons so thrown together, but each is apt to regard such new acquaintance merely as bearing upon his or her own particular interests. It is surprising to see how people will live side by side in solitude, even in danger, in distant settlements, in the mining districts of the West, in up-country stations in India, on board ship, even, for months and years, without knowing anything of each other's previous history; whereas in the crowded centres of civilisation and society the first questions are " Where does he come from ?" " What are his antecedents ?" " What has he done in the world ?"   And unless a man can answer such inquiries to the general satisfaction he is likely to be heavily handicapped in the social race.   But in more primitive situations men are ruled by more primitive feelings of mutual respect; it is considered that a man should not be pressed to speak of things he shows no desire to discuss and that, provided he does not interfere with his neighbour's wellbeing, his past life is nobody's business.   One may feel curiosity concerning him, but under no circumstances is one justified in asking questions.

For these reasons, although Mr. Juxon's arrival and instalment in the Hall were regarded with satisfaction by the little circle at Billingsfield, while he himself was at once received into intimacy and treated with cordial friendliness, he nevertheless represented in the minds of all an unsolved enigma.   And to the squire the existence of one of the circle was at least as problematical as his own life could seem to any

of them. The more he saw of Mrs. Goddard,
the more he wondered at her and speculated
about her and the less he dared to ask her any
questions. But he understood from Mr. Ambrose's
manner, that the vicar at least was in possession
of her secret, and he inferred from what he was
able to judge about the vicar's character that the
latter was not a man to extend his friendship to
any one who did not deserve it. Whatever Mrs.
Goddard's story was, he felt sure that her troubles
had not been caused by her own misconduct.
She was in every respect what he called a good
woman. Of course, too, she was a widow; the
way in which she spoke of her husband implied
that, on those rare occasions when she spoke of
him at all. Charles James Juxon was a
gentleman, whatever course of life he had
followed before settling in the country, and he
did not feel that he should be justified in asking
questions about Mrs. Goddard of the vicar.
Besides, as time went on and he found his own
interest in her increasing, he began to nourish
the hope that he might one day hear her story
from her own lips. In his simplicity it did not

strike him that he himself had grown to be an object of interest to her.

Somehow, during the summer and autumn of that year, Mrs. Goddard contracted a habit of watching the park gate from the window of the cottage, particularly at certain hours of the day. It was only a habit, but it seemed to amuse her. She used to sit in the small bay window with her books, reading to herself or teaching Nellie, and it was quite natural that from time to time she should look out across the road. But it rarely happened, when she was installed in that particular place, that Mr. Juxon failed to appear at the gate, with his dog Stamboul, his green stockings, his stick and the inevitable rose in his coat. Moreover he generally crossed the road and, if he did not enter the cottage and spend a quarter of an hour in conversation, he at least spoke to Mrs. Goddard through the open window. It was remarkable, too, that as time went on what at first had seemed the result of chance, recurred with such invariable regularity as to betray the existence of a fixed rule. Nellie, too, who was an observant child, had ceased asking questions but watched her mother with her great violet eyes in a way that made Mrs. Goddard nervous. Nellie liked the squire very much but though she asked her mother very often at first whether she, too, was fond of that nice Mr. Juxon, the answers she received were not encouraging. How was it possible, Mrs. Goddard asked, to speak of liking anybody one had known so short a time? And as Nellie was quite unable to answer such an inquiry, she desisted from her questions and applied herself to the method of personal observation. But here, too, she was met by a hopeless difficulty. The squire and her mother never seemed to have any secrets, as Nellie would have expressed it. They met daily, and daily exchanged very much the same remarks concerning the weather, the garden, the vicar's last sermon. When they talked about anything else, they spoke of books, of which the squire lent Mrs. Goddard a great number. But this was a subject which did not interest Nellie very much; she was not by any means a prodigy in the way of learning, and though she was now nearly eleven years old was only just beginning to read the Waverley novels. On one occasion she remarked to her mother that she did not believe a word of them and did not think they were a bit like real life, but the momentary fit of scepticism soon passed and Nellie read on contentedly, not omitting however to watch her mother in order to find out, as her small mind expressed it, " whether mamma really liked that nice Mr. Juxon." Events were slowly preparing themselves which would help her to come to a satisfactory conclusion upon that matter.

Mr. Juxon himself was in a very uncertain state of mind. After knowing Mrs. Goddard for six months, and having acquired the habit of seeing her almost every day, he found to his surprise that she formed a necessary part of his existence. It need not have surprised him, for in spite of that lady's surmise with regard to his early life, he was in reality a man of generous and susceptible temperament. He recognised in the charming tenant of the cottage many qualities which he liked, and he could not deny that she was exceedingly pretty. Being a strong man he was particularly attracted by the pathetic expression of her face, the perpetual sadness that was visible there when she was not momentarily interested or amused. Had he suspected her paleness and air of secret suffering to be the result of any physical infirmity, she would not have interested him so much. But Mrs. Goddard's lithe figure and easy grace of activity belied all idea of weakness. It was undoubtedly some hidden suffering of mind which lent that sadness to her voice and features, and which so deeply roused the sympathies of the squire. At the end of six months Mr. Juxon was very much interested in Mrs. Goddard, but despite all his efforts to be agreeable he seemed to have made no progress whatever in the direction of banishing her cares. To tell the truth, it did not enter his mind that he was in love with her. She was his tenant; she was evidently very unhappy about something; it was therefore undeniably his duty as a landlord and as a gentleman to make life easy for her.

He wondered what the matter could be. At first he had been inclined to think that she was poor and was depressed by poverty. But though she lived very simply, she never seemed to be in difficulties. Five hundred pounds a year go a long way in the village of Billingsfield. It was certainly not want of money which made her unhappy. The interest of the sum represented by the pictures hung in her little sitting-room, not to mention the other objects of value she possessed, would have been alone sufficient to afford her a living. The squire himself would have given her a high price for these things, but in six months she never in the most distant manner suggested that she wished to part with them. The idea then naturally suggested itself to Mr. Juxon's mind that she was still mourning for her husband, and that she would probably continue to mourn for him until some one, himself for instance, succeeded in consoling her for so great a loss.

The conclusion startled the squire. That was not precisely the part he contemplated playing, nor the species of consolation he proposed to offer. Mrs. Goddard was indeed a charming woman, and the squire liked charming women and delighted in their society. But Mr. Juxon was a bachelor of more than forty years standing, and he had never regarded marriage as a thing of itself, for himself, desirable. He immediately thrust the idea from his mind with a mental "*vade retro Satanas!*" and determined that things were very agreeable in their present state, and might go on for ever; that if Mrs. Goddard was unhappy that did not prevent her from talking very pleasantly whenever he saw her, which was nearly every day, and that her griefs were emphatically none of his business. Before very long however Mr. Juxon discovered that though it was a very simple thing to make such a determination it was a very different thing to keep it. Mrs. Goddard interested him too much. When he was with her he was perpetually longing to talk about herself instead of about the weather and the garden and the books, and once or twice he was very nearly betrayed into talking about himself, a circumstance so extraordinary that Mr. Juxon imagined he must be either ill or going mad, and thought seriously of sending for the doctor. He controlled the impulse, however, and temporarily recovered; but strange to say from that time forward the conversation languished when he found himself alone with Mrs. Goddard, and it seemed very hard to maintain their joint interest in the weather, the garden and the books at the proper standard of intensity. They had grown intimate, and familiarity had begun to breed a contempt of those petty subjects upon which their intimacy had been founded. It is not clear why this should be so, but it is true, nevertheless, and many a couple before Charles Juxon and Mary Goddard had found it out. As the interest of two people in each other increases their interest in things, as things, diminishes in like ratio, and they are very certain ultimately to reach that point described by the Frenchman's maxim—"a man should never talk to a woman except of herself or himself."

If Mr. Juxon was not in love with Mary Goddard he was at least rapidly approaching a very dangerous state; for he saw her every day and could not let one day go by without seeing her, and moreover he grew silent in her company,

to a degree which embarrassed her and made
him feel himself more stupid than he had ever
dreamed possible ; so that he would sometimes
stay too long, in the hope of finding something
to say, and sometimes he would leave her
abruptly and go and shut himself up with his
books, and busy himself with his catalogues and
his bindings and the arrangement of his rare
editions. One day at last, he felt that he had
behaved so very absurdly that he was ashamed
of himself, and suddenly disappeared for nearly
a week. When he returned he said he had
been to town to attend a great sale of books,
which was perfectly true ; he did not add that
the learned expert he employed in London could
have done the business for him just as well.
But the trip had done him no good, for he grew
more silent than ever, and Mrs. Goddard even
thought his brown face looked a shade paler
but that might have been the effect of the winter
weather. Ordinary sunburn she reflected, as she
looked at her own white skin in the mirror, will
generally wear off in six months, though freckles
will not.

If Mr. Juxon was not in love, it would be very hard to say what Mary Goddard felt. It was not true that time was effacing the memory of the great sorrow she had suffered. It was there still, that memory, keen and sharp as ever; it would never go away again so long as she lived. But she had been soothed by the quiet life in Billingsfield; the evidences of the past had been removed far from her, she had found in the Reverend Augustin Ambrose one of those rare and manly natures who can keep a secret for ever without ever referring to its existence even with the person who has confided it. For a few days she had hesitated whether to ask the vicar's advice about Mr. Juxon or not. She had thought it her duty to allow Mr. Ambrose to tell the squire whatever he thought fit of her own story. But she had changed her mind, and the squire had remained in ignorance. It was best so, she thought; for now, after more than six months, Mr. Juxon had taken the position of a friend towards her, and, as she thought, showed no disposition whatever to overstep the boundaries of friendship. The regularity of his visits and

the sameness of the conversation seemed of themselves a guarantee of his simple goodwill. It
did not strike her as possible that if he were
going to fall in love with her at all, that catas-
.trophe should be postponed beyond six months
from their first acquaintance. Nor did it seem
extraordinary to her that she should actually
look forward to those visits, and take pleasure
in that monotonous intercourse. Her life was
very quiet; it was natural that she should take
whatever diversion came in her way, and should
even be thankful for it. Mr. Juxon was an
honest gentleman, a scholar and a man who had
seen the world. If what he said was not always
very original it was always very true, a merit
not always conceded to the highest originality.
He spoke intelligently; he told her the news;
he lent her the newest books and reviews, and
offered her his opinions upon them, with the
regularity of a daily paper. In such a place,
where communications with the outer world
seemed as difficult as at the antipodes, and
where the remainder of society was limited to
the household of the vicarage, what wonder

was it if she found Mr. Juxon an agreeable companion, and believed the companionship harmless?

But far down in the involutions of her feminine consciousness there was present a perpetual curiosity in regard to the squire, a curiosity she never expected to satisfy, but was wholly unable to repress. Under the influence of this feeling she made remarks from time to time of an apparently harmless nature, but which in the squire promoted that strange inclination to talk about himself, which he had lately observed and which caused him so much alarm. He said to himself that he had nothing to be concealed, and that if any one had asked him direct questions concerning his past he would have answered them boldly enough. But he knew himself to be so singularly averse to dwelling on his own affairs that he wondered why he should now be impelled to break through so good a rule. Indeed he had not the insight to perceive that Mrs. Goddard lost no opportunity of leading him to the subject of his various adventures, and, if he had suspected it, he would have been very much surprised.

Mr. and Mrs. Ambrose were far from guessing what an intimacy had sprung up between the two. Both the cottage and the Hall lay at a considerable distance from the vicarage, and though Mrs. Ambrose occasionally went to see Mrs. Goddard at irregular hours in the morning and afternoon, it was remarkable that the squire never called when she was there. Once Mrs. Ambrose arrived during one of his visits, but thought it natural enough that Mr. Juxon should drop in to see his tenant. Indeed when she called the two were talking about the garden —as usual.

CHAPTER VI.

JOHN SHORT had almost finished his hard work
at college. For two years and a half he had
laboured on acquiring for himself reputation and
a certain amount of more solid advantage in the
shape of scholarships. Never in that time had
he left Cambridge even for a day unless com-
pelled to do so by the regulations of his college.
His father had found it hard to induce him to
come up to town ; and, being in somewhat easier
circumstances since John had declared that he
needed no further help to complete his education, he had himself gone to see his son more
than once. But John had never been to Billingsfield and he knew nothing of the changes
that had taken place there. At last, however,
Short felt that he must have some rest before
he went up for honours ; he had grown thin and

even pale; his head ached perpetually, and his eyes no longer seemed so good as they had been. He went to a doctor, and the doctor told him that with his admirable constitution a few days of absolute rest would do all that was necessary. John wrote to Mr. Ambrose to say that he would at last accept the invitation so often extended and would spend the week between Christmas and New Year's day at Billingsfield.

There were great rejoicings at the vicarage. John had never been forgotten for a day since he had left, each successive step in his career had been hailed with hearty delight, and now that at last he was coming back to rest himself for a week before the final effort Mrs. Ambrose was as enthusiastic as her husband. Even Mrs. Goddard who was not quite sure whether she had ever seen John or not, and the squire who had certainly never seen him, joined in the general excitement. Mrs. Goddard asked the entire party to tea at the cottage and the squire asked them to come and skate at the Hall and to dine afterwards; for the weather was cold and the vicar said John was a very good skater. Was there anything

John could not do? There was nothing he could not do much better than anybody else, answered Mr. Ambrose; and the good clergyman's pride in his pupil was perhaps not the less because he had at first received him on charitable considerations, and felt that if he had risked much in being so generous he had also been amply rewarded by the brilliant success of his undertaking.

When John arrived, everybody said he was "so much improved." He had got his growth now, being close upon one and twenty years of age; his blue eyes were deeper set; his downy whiskers had disappeared and a small moustache shaded his upper lip; he looked more intellectual but not less strong, though Mrs. Ambrose said he was dreadfully pale—perhaps he owed some of the improvement observed in his appearance to the clothes he wore. Poor boy, he had been but scantily supplied in the old days; he looked prosperous, now, by comparison.

"We have had great additions to our society, since you left us," said the vicar. "We have got a squire at the Hall, and a lady with a little girl at the cottage."

"Such a nice little girl" remarked Mrs. Ambrose.

When John found out that the lady at the cottage was no other than the lady in black to whom he had lost his heart two years and a half before, he was considerably surprised. It would be absurd to suppose that the boyish fancy which had made so much romance in his life for so many months could outlast the excitements of the University. It would be absurd to dignify such a fancy by any serious name. He had grown to be a man since those days and he had put away childish things. He blushed to remember that he had spent hours in writing odes to the beautiful unknown, and whole nights in dreaming of her face. And yet he could remember that as much as a year after he had left Billingsfield he still thought of her as his highest ideal of woman, and still occasionally composed a few verses to her memory, regretting, perhaps, the cooling of his poetic ardour. Then he had gradually lost sight of her in the hard work which made up his life. Profound study had made him more prosaic and he believed that he had done with ideals for ever after the manner of many clever young fellows who at one and twenty feel that they are separated from the follies of eighteen by a great and impassable gulf. The gulf, however, was not in John's case so wide nor so deep but what, at the prospect of being suddenly brought face to face, and made acquainted, with her who for so long had seemed the object of a romantic passion, he felt a strange thrill of surprise and embarrassment. Those meetings of later years generally bring painful disillusion. How many of us can remember some fair-haired little girl who in our childhood represented to us the very incarnation of feminine grace and beauty, for whom we fetched and carried, for whom we bound nosegays on the heath and stole apples from the orchard and climbed upon the table after desert, if we were left alone in the dining-room, to lay hands on some beautiful sweetmeat wrapped in tinsel and fringes of pink paper—have we not met her again in after-life, a grown woman, very, very far from our ideal of feminine grace and beauty? And still in spite of changes in herself and ourselves there has clung to her memory through all those years enough of romance to make our heart beat a little faster at the prospect of suddenly meeting her, enough to make us wonder a little regretfully if she was at all like the little golden-haired child we loved long ago.

But with John the feeling was stronger than that. It was but two years and a half since he had seen Mrs. Goddard, and, not even knowing her name, had erected for her a pedestal in his boyish heart. There was moreover about her a mystery still unsolved. There was something odd and strange in her one visit to the vicarage, in the fact that the vicar had never referred to that visit and, lastly, it seemed unlike Mr. Ambrose to have said nothing of her settlement in Billingsfield in the course of all the letters he had written to John since the latter had left him. John dwelt upon the name—Goddard—but it held no association for him. It was not at all like the names he had given her in his imagination. He wondered what she would be like and he felt nervously anxious to meet her. Somehow, too, what he heard of the squire did not please him; he felt an immediate antagonism to Mr. Juxon, to his books, to his amateur scholarship, even to his appearance as described by Mrs. Ambrose, who said he was such a thorough Englishman and wondered how he kept his hair so smooth.

It was not long before he had an opportunity of judging for himself of what Mr. Ambrose called the recent addition to Billingsfield society. On the very afternoon of his arrival the vicar proposed to walk up to the Hall and have a look at the library, and John readily assented. It was Christmas Eve and the weather, even in Essex, was sharp and frosty. The muddy road was frozen hard and the afternoon sun, slanting through the oak trees that bordered the road beyond the village, made no perceptible impression on the cold. The two men walked briskly in the direction of the park gate. Before they had quite reached it however, the door of the cottage opposite was opened, and Stamboul, the Russian bloodhound, bounded down the path cleared the wicket gate in his vast stride, and then turning suddenly crouched in the middle of the road to wait for his master. But the dog instantly caught sight of the vicar, with whom he was on very good terms, and trotted slowly up to him, thrusting his great nose into his hand, and then proceeding to make acquaintance with John. He seemed to approve of the stranger, for he gave a short sniff of satisfaction and trotted back to the wicket of the cottage. At this moment Mrs. Goddard and Nellie came out, followed by the squire arrayed in his inevitable green stockings. There was however no rose in his coat. Whether the greenhouses at the Hall had failed to produce any in the bitter weather, or whether Mr. Juxon had transferred the rose from his coat to the possession of Mrs. Goddard, is uncertain. The three came out into the road where the vicar and John stood still to meet them.

"Mrs. Goddard," said the clergyman, "this is Mr. Short, of whom you have heard—John, let me introduce you to Mr. Juxon."

John felt that he blushed violently as he took Mrs. Goddard's hand. He would not have believed that he could feel so much embarrassed, and he hated himself for betraying it. But nobody noticed his colour. The weather was bright and cold, and even Mrs. Goddard's pale and delicate skin had a rosy tinge.

"We were just going for a walk," she explained.

"And we were going to see you at the Hall," said the vicar to Mr. Juxon.

"Let us do both," said the latter. "Let us walk to the Hall and have a cup of tea. We can look at the ice and see whether it will bear to-morrow."

Everybody agreed to the proposal, and it so fell out that the squire and the vicar went before while John and Mrs. Goddard followed and Nellie walked between them, holding Stamboul by the collar, and talking to him as she went. John looked at his companion, and saw with a strange satisfaction that his first impression, the impression he had cherished so long, had not been a mistaken one. Her deep violet eyes were still sad, beautiful and dreamy. Her small nose was full of expression, and was not reddened by the cold as noses are wont to be. Her rich brown hair waved across her forehead as it did on that day when John first saw her; and now as he spoke with her, her mouth smiled, as he had been sure it would.   John felt a curious sense of pride in her, in finding that he had not been deceived, that this ideal of whom he had dreamed was really and truly very good to look at.   He knew little of the artist's rules of beauty; he had often looked with wonder at the faces in the illustrations to Dr. Smith's classical dictionary, and had tried to understand where the beauty of them lay, and at Cambridge he had seen and studied with interest many photographs and casts from the antiques.   But to his mind the antique would not bear comparison for a moment with Mrs. Goddard, who resembled no engraving nor photograph nor cast he had ever seen.

And she, too, looked at him, and said to herself that he did not look like what she had expected. He looked like a lean, fresh young Englishman of moderate intelligence and in moderate circumstances.   And yet she knew that he was no ordinary young fellow, that he was wonderfully gifted, in fact, and likely to make a mark in the world.   She resolved to take a proper interest in him.

"Do you know," she said, " I have heard so

much about you, that I feel as though I had met you before, Mr. Short."

"We really have met," said John. "Do you remember that hot day when you came to the vicarage and I waked up Muggins for you?"

"Yes—was that you? You have changed. That is, I suppose I did not see you very well in the hurry."

"I suppose I have changed in two years and a half. I was only a boy then, you know. But how have you heard so much about me?"

"Billingsfield," said Mrs. Goddard with a faint smile, "is not a large place. The Ambroses are very fond of you and always talk of what you are doing."

"And so you really live here, Mrs. Goddard? How long is it since you came? Mr. Ambrose never told me——"

"I have been here more than two years—two years last October," she answered quietly.

"The very year I left—only a month after I was gone. How strange!"

Mrs. Goddard looked up nervously. She was frightened lest John should have made any deductions from the date of her arrival. But John was thinking in a very different train of thought.

"Why is it strange?" she asked.

"Oh, I hardly know," said John in considerable embarrassment. "I was only thinking—about you—that is, about it all."

The answer did not tend to quiet Mrs. Goddard's apprehensions.

"About me?" she exclaimed. "Why should you think about me?"

"It was very foolish, of course," said John. "Only, when I caught sight of you that day I was very much struck. You know, I was only a boy, then. I hoped you would come back— but you did not." He blushed violently, and then glanced at his companion to see whether she had noticed it.

"No," she said, "I did not come back for some time."

"And then I was gone. Mr. Ambrose never told me you had come."

"Why should he?"

"Oh, I don't know. I think he might. You see Billingsfield has been a sort of home to me and it is a small place; so I thought he might have told me the news."

"I suppose he thought it would not interest you," said Mrs. Goddard. "I am sure I do not know why it should. But you must be very fond of the place, are you not?"

"Very. As I was saying, it is very like home to me. My father lives in town you know—that is not at all like home. One always associates the idea of home with the country, and a vicarage and a Hall, and all that."

"Does one?" said Mrs. Goddard, picking her way over the frozen mud of the road. "Take care, Nellie, it is dreadfully slippery!"

"How much she has grown," remarked John, looking at the girl's active figure as she walked before them. "She was quite a little girl when I saw her first."

"Yes, she grows very fast," answered Mrs. Goddard rather regretfully.

"You say that as though you were sorry."

"I? No. I am glad to see her grow. What a funny remark."

"I thought you spoke sadly," explained John.

"Oh, dear no. Only she is coming to the awkward age."

"She is coming to it very gracefully," said John, who wanted to say something pleasant.

"That is the most any of us can hope to do," answered Mrs. Goddard with a little smile. "We all have our awkward age, I suppose."

"I should not think you could remember yours."

"Why? Do you think it was so very long ago?" Mrs. Goddard laughed.

"No—I cannot believe you ever had any," said John.

The boyish compliment pleased Mrs. Goddard. It was long since any one had flattered her, for flattery did not enter into the squire's system for making himself agreeable.

"Do they teach that sort of thing at Cambridge?" she asked demurely.

"What sort of thing?"

"Making little speeches to ladies," said she.

"No—I wish they did," said John, laughing. "I should know much better how to make them. We learn how to write Greek odes to moral abstractions."

"What a dreadful thing to do!" exclaimed Mrs. Goddard.

"Do you think so? I do not know. Now, for instance, I have written a great many Greek odes to you——"

"To me?" interrupted his companion in surprise.

"Do you think it is so very extraordinary?"

"Very."

"Well—you see—I only saw you once—you won't laugh?"

"No," said Mrs. Goddard, who was very much amused, and was beginning to think that John Short was the most original young man she had ever met.

"I only saw you once, when you came to the vicarage, and I had not the least idea what your name was. But I—I hoped you would come back; and so I used to write poems to you. They were very good, too," added John in a meditative tone, "I have never written any nearly so good as they were."

"Really?" Mrs. Goddard looked at him rather incredulously and then laughed.

"You said you would not laugh," objected John.

"I cannot help it in the least," said she. "It seems so funny."

"It did not seem funny to me, I can assure you," replied John rather warmly. "I thought it very serious."

"You don't do it now, do you?" asked Mrs. Goddard, looking up at him quietly.

"Oh no—a man's ideals change so much, you know," answered John, who felt he had been foolishly betrayed into telling his story, and hated to be laughed at.

"I am very glad of that. How long are you going to stay here, Mr. Short?"

"Until New Year's Day, I think," he answered. "Perhaps you will have time to forget about the poetry before I go."

"I don't know why," said Mrs. Goddard, noticing his hurt tone. "I think it was very pretty—I mean the way you did it. You must be a born poet—to write verses to a person you did not know and had only seen once!"

"It is much easier than writing verses to

moral abstractions one has never seen at all," explained John, who was easily pacified. "When a man writes a great deal he feels the necessity of attaching all those beautiful moral qualities to some real, living person whom he can see——"

"Even if he only sees her once," remarked Mrs. Goddard demurely.

"Yes, even if he only sees her once. You have no idea how hard it is to concentrate one's faculties upon a mere idea; but the moment a man sees a woman whom he can endow with all sorts of beautiful qualities—why it's just as easy as hunting."

"I am glad to have been of so much service to you, even unconsciously—but, don't you think perhaps Mrs. Ambrose would have done as well?"

"Mrs. Ambrose?" repeated John. Then he broke into a hearty laugh. "No—I have no hesitation in saying that she would not have done as well. I am deeply indebted to Mrs. Ambrose for a thousand kindnesses, for a great deal more than I can tell—but, on the whole, I say, no ; I could not have written odes to Mrs. Ambrose."

"No, I suppose not. Besides, fancy the vicar's state of mind ! She would have had to call him in to translate your poetry."

"It is very singular," said John in a tone of reflection. "But, if I had not done all that, we should not be talking as we are now, after ten minutes acquaintance."

"Probably not," said Mrs. Goddard.

"No—certainly not. By the bye, there is the Hall. I suppose you have often been there since Mr. Juxon came—what kind of man is he ? "

"He has been a great traveller," answered his companion. "And then—well, he is a scholar and has an immense library——"

"And an immense dog—yes, but I mean' what kind of man is he himself ? "

"He is very agreeable," said Mrs. Goddard quietly. "Very well bred, very well educated. We find him a great addition in Billingsfield."

"I should think so, if he is all you say," said John discontentedly. His antagonism against Mr. Juxon was rapidly increasing. Mrs. Goddard looked at him in some surprise, being very far from understanding his tone.

"I think you will like him," she said. "He knows all about you from the Ambroses, and he always speaks of you with the greatest admiration."

"Really? It is awfully kind of him, I am sure. I am very much obliged," said John rather contemptuously.

"Why do you speak like that?" asked Mrs. Goddard gravely. "You cannot possibly have any cause for disliking him. Besides, he is a friend of ours——"

"Oh, of course, then it is different," said John. "If he is a friend of yours——"

"Do you generally take violent dislikes to people at first sight, Mr. Short?"

"Oh, dear no. Not at all—at least, not dislikes. I suppose Mr. Juxon's face reminds me of somebody I do not like. I will behave like an angel. Here we are."

The effect of this conversation upon the two persons between whom it took place was exceedingly different. Mrs. Goddard was amused, with-

out being altogether pleased. She had made
the acquaintance of a refreshingly young scholar
whom she understood to be full of genius. He
was enthusiastic, simple, seemingly incapable of
concealing anything that passed through his mind,
unreasonable and evidently very susceptible. On
the whole, she thought she should like him,
though his scornful manner in speaking of the
squire had annoyed her. The interest she could
feel in him, if she felt any at all, would be akin
to that of the vicar in the boy. He was only
a boy; brilliantly talented, they said, but still
a mere boy. She was fully ten years older than
he—she might almost be his mother—well, not
quite that, but very nearly. It was amusing to
think of his writing odes to her. She wished
she could see translations of them, and she almost
made up her mind to ask him to show them to her.

John on the other hand experienced a curious
sensation. He had never before been in the
society of so charming a woman. He looked at
her and looked again, and came to the conclusion
that she was not only charming but beautiful.
He had not the least idea of her age; it is not

the manner of his kind to think much about the age of a woman, provided she is not too young. The girl might be ten. Mrs. Goddard might have married at sixteen—twenty-six, twenty-seven—what was that? John called himself twenty-two. Five years was simply no difference at all! Besides, who cared for age?

He had suddenly found himself almost on a footing of intimacy with this lovely creature. His odes had served him well; it had pleased her to hear the story. She had laughed a little, of course; but women, as John knew, always laugh when they are pleased. He would like to show her his odes. As he walked through the park by her side he felt a curious sense of possession in her which gave him a thrill of exquisite delight; and when they entered the Hall he felt as though he were resigning her to the squire, which gave him a corresponding sense of annoyance. When an Englishman experiences these sensations, he is in love. John resolved that whatever happened he would walk back with Mrs. Goddard.

" Come in," said the squire cheerily. " We are not so cold as we used to be up here."

A great fire of logs was burning upon the hearth in the Hall. Stamboul stalked up to the open chimney, scratched the tiger's skin which served for a rug, and threw himself down as though his day's work were done. Mr. Juxon went up to Mrs. Goddard.

"I think you had better take off your coat," he said. "The house is very warm."

Mrs. Goddard allowed the squire to help her in removing the heavy black jacket lined and trimmed with fur, which she wore. John eyed the proceeding uneasily and kept on his great-coat.

"Thank you—I don't mind the heat," he said shortly when the squire suggested to him that he might be too warm. John was in a fit of contrariety. Mrs. Goddard glanced at him, as he spoke, and he thought he detected a twinkle of amusement in her eyes, which did not tend to smooth his temper.

"You will have some tea, Mrs. Goddard?" said Mr. Juxon, leading the way into the library, which he regarded as the most habitable room in the house. Mrs. Goddard walked by his side and the vicar followed, while John and Nellie brought up the rear.

"Is not it a beautiful place?" said Nellie, who was anxious that the new-comer should appreciate the magnificence of the Hall.

"Can't see very well," said John, "it is so dark."

"Oh, but it is beautiful," insisted Miss Nellie. "And they have lots of lamps here in the evening. Perhaps Mr. Juxon will have them lighted before we go. He is always so kind."

"Is he?" asked John with a show of interest.

"Yes—he brings mamma a rose every day," said Nellie.

"Not really?" said John, beginning to feel that he was justified in hating the squire with all his might.

"Yes—and books, too. Lots of them—but then, he has so many. See, this is the library. Is not it splendid!"

John looked about him and was surprised. The last rays of the setting sun fell across the open lawn and through the deep windows of the great room, illuminating the tall carved bookcases, the heavily gilt bindings, the rich, dark Russia leather and morocco of the folios. The footsteps of the party fell noiselessly upon the thick carpet and almost insensibly the voices of the visitors dropped to a lower key. A fine large wood fire was burning on the hearth, carefully covered with a metal netting lest any spark should fly out and cause damage to the treasures accumulated in the neighbouring shelves.

"Pray make yourself at home, Mr. Short," said the squire, coming up to John. "You may find something of interest here. There are some old editions of the classics that are thought rare —some specimens of Venetian printing, too, that you may like to look at. Mr. Ambrose can tell you more about them than I."

John's feeling of antagonism, and even his resentment against Mr. Juxon, roused by Nellie's innocent remark about the roses, were not proof against the real scholastic passion aroused by the sight of rare and valuable books. In a few minutes he had divested himself of his great coat and was examining the books with an expression of delight upon his face which was pleasant to see.   He glanced from time to time at the other persons in the room and looked very often at Mrs. Goddard, but on the whole he was profoundly interested in the contents of the library.   Mrs. Goddard was installed in a huge leathern easy-chair by the fire, and the squire was handing her one after another a number of new volumes which lay upon a small table, and which she appeared to examine with interest. Nellie knew where to look for her favourite books of engravings and had curled herself up in a corner absorbed in "Hyde's Royal Residences." The vicar went to look for something he wanted to consult.

"What do you think of our new friend?" asked Mrs. Goddard of the squire.   She spoke in a low tone and did not look up from the new book he had just handed her.

"He appears to have a very peculiar temper," said Mr. Juxon.   "But he looks clever."

"What do you think he was talking about we as came through the park?" asked Mrs. Goddard.

"What?"

"He was saying that he saw me once before he went to college, and—fancy how deliciously boyish! he said he had written ever so many Greek odes to my memory since!" Mrs. Goddard laughed a little and blushed faintly.

"Let us hope, for the sake of his success, that you may continue to inspire him," said the squire gravely. "I have no doubt the odes were very good."

"So he said.   Fancy!"

CHAPTER VII.

Mrs. Goddard did not mean to walk home with John; but on the other hand she did not mean to walk with the squire. She revolved the matter in her mind as she sat in the library talking in an undertone with Mr. Juxon. She liked the great room, the air of luxury, the squire's tea and the squire's conversation. It is worth noticing that his flow of talk was more abundant to-day than it had been for some time; whether it was John's presence which stimulated Mr. Juxon's imagination, or whether Mrs. Goddard had suddenly grown more interesting since John Short's appearance it is hard to say; it is certain that Mr. Juxon talked better than usual.

The afternoon, however, was far spent and the party had only come to make a short visit. Mrs. Goddard rose from her seat.

"Nellie, child, we must be going home," she said, calling to the little girl who was still absorbed in the book of engravings which she had taken to the window to catch the last of the waning light.

John started and came forward with alacrity. The vicar looked up; Nellie reluctantly brought her book back.

"It is very early," objected the squire. "Really, the days have no business to be so short."

"It would not seem like Christmas if they were long," said Mrs. Goddard.

"It does not seem like Christmas anyhow," remarked John, enigmatically. No one understood his observation and no one paid any attention to it. Whereupon John's previous feeling of annoyance returned and he went to look for his greatcoat in the dark corner where he had laid it.

"You must not come all the way back with us," said Mrs. Goddard as they all went out into the hall and began to put on their warm things before the fire. "Really—it is late. Mr. Ambrose will give me his arm."

The squire insisted however, and Stamboul, who had had a comfortable nap by the fire, was of the same opinion as his master and plunged wildly at the door.

"Will you give me your arm, Mr. Ambrose ?" said Mrs. Goddard, looking rather timidly at the vicar as they stood upon the broad steps in the sparkling evening air. She felt that she was disappointing both the squire and John, but she had quite made up her mind. She had her own reasons. The vicar, good man, was unconsciously a little flattered by her choice, as with her hand resting on the sleeve of his greatcoat he led the way down the park. The squire and John were fain to follow together, but Nellie took her mother's hand, and Stamboul walked behind affecting an unusual gravity.

"You must come again when there is more daylight," said Mr. Juxon to his companion.

"Thank you," said John. "You are very good." He intended to relapse into silence, but his instinct made him ashamed of seeming rude. "You have a magnificent library," he added presently in a rather cold tone.

"You have been used to much better ones in Cambridge," said the squire, modestly.

"Do you know Cambridge well, Mr. Juxon?"

"Very well.   I am a Cambridge man, myself."

"Indeed?" exclaimed John, immediately discovering that the squire was not so bad as he had thought. "Indeed! I had no idea. Mr. Ambrose never told me that."

"I am not sure that he is aware of it," said Mr. Juxon quietly. "The subject never happened to come up."

"How odd!" remarked John, who could not conceive of associating with a man for any length of time without asking at what University he had been.

"I don't know," answered Mr. Juxon. "There are lots of other things to talk about."

"Oh—of course," said John, in a tone which did not express conviction.

Meanwhile Mr. Ambrose and Mrs. Goddard walked briskly in front; so briskly in fact that Nellie occasionally jumped a step, as children say, in order to keep up with them.

"What a glorious Christmas eve!" exclaimed

Mrs. Goddard, as they turned a bend in the drive and caught sight of the western sky still clear and red. "And there is the new moon!" The slender crescent was hanging just above the fading glow.

"Oh mamma, have you wished?" cried Nellie. "You must, you know, when you see the new moon!"

Mrs. Goddard did not answer, but she sighed faintly and drew a little closer to the worthy vicar as she walked. She always wished, whether there was a new moon or not, and she always wished the same wish. Perhaps Mr. Ambrose understood, for he was not without tact. He changed the subject.

"How do you like our John Short?" he asked.

"Very much, I think," answered Mrs. Goddard. "He is so fresh and young."

"He is a fine fellow. I was sure you would like him. Is he at all like what you fancied he would be?"

"Well no——not exactly. I know you told me how he looked, but I always thought he would be rather Byronic—the poetical type, if you know what I mean."

"He has a great deal of poetry in him," said Mr. Ambrose in a tone of profound admiration. "He writes the best Greek verse I ever saw."

"Oh yes—I daresay," replied Mrs. Goddard smiling in the dusk. "I am sure he must be very clever."

So they chatted quietly as they walked down the park. But the squire and John did not make progress in their conversation, and by the time they reached the gate they had yielded to an awkward silence. They had both been annoyed because Mrs. Goddard had taken the vicar's arm instead of choosing one of themselves, but the joint sense of disappointment did not constitute a common bond of interest. Either one would have suffered anything rather than mention Mrs. Goddard to the other in the course of the walk. And yet Mr. Juxon might have been John's father. At the gate of the cottage they separated. The squire said he would turn back. Mrs. Goddard had reached her destination. John and the vicar would return to the vicarage.

John tried to linger a moment, to get a word with Mrs. Goddard. He was so persistent that she let him follow her through the wicket gate and then turned quickly.

"What is it?" she asked, rather suddenly, holding out her hand to say good-bye.

"Oh, nothing," answered John. "That is— would you like to see one of those—those little odes of mine?"

"Yes, certainly, if you like," she answered frankly, and then laughed. "Of course I would. Goodnight."

He turned and fled. The vicar was waiting for him, and eyed him rather curiously as he came back. Mr. Juxon was standing in the middle of the road, making Stamboul jump over his stick, backwards and forwards.

"Good-night," he said, pausing in his occupation. The vicar and John turned away and walked homewards. Before they turned the corner towards the village John instinctively looked back. Mr. Juxon was still making Stamboul jump the stick before the cottage, but as far as he could see in the dusk, Mrs. Goddard and Nellie had disappeared within. John felt that he was very unhappy.

"Mr. Ambrose," he began. Then he stopped and hesitated. "Mr. Ambrose," he continued at last, "you never told me half the news of Billingsfield in your letters."

"You mean about Mrs. Goddard? Well—no—I did not think it would interest you very much."

"She is a very interesting person," said John. He could have added that if he had known she was in Billingsfield he would have made a great sacrifice in order to come down for a day to make her acquaintance. But he did not say it.

"She is a great addition," said the vicar.

"Oh—very great, I should think."

Christmas eve was passed at the vicarage in preparation for the morrow. Mrs. Ambrose was very active in binding holly wherever it was possible to put it. The mince-pies were tasted and pronounced a success, and old Reynolds was despatched to the cottage with a small basket containing a certain number of them as a present to Mrs. Goddard. An emissary appeared from the Hall with a variety of articles which the squire begged to contribute towards the vicar's Christmas dinner; among others a haunch of venison which Mrs. Ambrose pronounced to be in the best condition. The vicar retorted by sending to the Hall a magnificent Cottenham cheese which, as a former Fellow of Trinity, he had succeeded in obtaining. Moreover Mr. Ambrose himself descended to the cellar and brought up several bottles of Audit ale which he declared must be allowed to stand some time in the pantry in order to bring out the flavour and to be thoroughly settled. John gave his assistance wherever it was needed and enjoyed vastly the old-fashioned preparations for Christmas day. It was long since the season had brought him such rejoicing and he intended to rejoice with a good will towards men and especially towards the Ambroses. After dinner the whole party, consisting of three highly efficient persons and old Reynolds, adjourned to the church to complete the decorations for the morrow.

The church of Billingsfield, known as St. Mary's, was quite large enough to contain twice

the entire population of the parish. It was built
upon a part of the foundations of an ancient
abbey, and the vicar was very proud of the
monument of a crusading Earl of Oxford which
he had caused to be placed in the chancel, it
having been discovered in the old chancel of the
abbey in the park, far beyond the present limits
of the church. The tower was the highest in
the neighbourhood. The whole building was of
gray rubble, irregular stones set together with a
crumbling cement, and presented an appearance
which, if not architecturally imposing, was at
least sufficiently venerable. At the present time
the aisles were full of heaped-up holly and
wreaths; a few lamps and a considerable number
of tallow candles shed a rather feeble light
amongst the pillars; a crowd of school children,
not yet washed for the morrow, were busy under
the directions of the schoolmistress in decorating
the chancel; Mr. Thomas Reid the conservative
sexton was at the top of a tall ladder, presum-
ably using doubtful language to himself as every
third nail he tried to drive into the crevices of
the stone " crooked hisself and larfed at him,"

as he expressed it; the organ was playing and a dozen small boys with three or four men were industriously practising the anthem "Arise, Shine," producing strains which if not calculated altogether to elevate the heart by their harmony, would certainly have caused the hair of a sensitive musician to rise on end; three or four of the oldest inhabitants were leaning on their sticks in the neighbourhood of the great stove in the middle aisle, warming themselves and grumbling that "times warn't as they used to be;" Mr. Abraham Boosey was noisily declaring that he had "cartlods more o' thim greens" to come, and Muggins, who had had some beer, was stumbling cheerfully against the pews in his efforts to bring a huge load of fir branches to the foot of Mr. Thomas Reid's long ladder. It was a thorough Christmas scene and John Short's heart warmed as he came back suddenly to the things which for three years had been so familiar to him and which he had so much missed in his solitude at Cambridge. Mr. and Mrs. Ambrose set to work and John followed their example. Even the prickly holly leaves were pleasant to touch and there was a homely joy in the fir branches dripping with half melted snow.

Before they had been at work very long, John was aware of a little figure, muffled in furs and standing beside him. He looked up and saw little Nellie's lovely face and long brown curls.

"Can't I help you, Mr. Short?" she asked timidly. "I like to help, and they won't let me."

"Who are 'they'?" asked John kindly, but looking about for the figure of Nellie's mother.

"The schoolmistress and Mrs. Ambrose. They said I should dirty my frock."

"Well," said John, doubtfully, "I don't know. Perhaps you would. But you might hold the string for me—that won't hurt your clothes, you know."

"There are more greens this year," remarked Nellie, sitting down upon the end of the choir bench where John was at work and taking the ball of string in her hand. "Mr. Juxon has sent a lot from the park."

"He seems to be always sending things," said John, who had no reason whatever for saying so, except that the squire had sent a hamper to the vicarage. "Did he stay long before dinner?" he added, in the tone people adopt when they hope to make children talk.

"Stay long where?" asked Nellie innocently.

"Oh, I thought he went into your house after we left you," answered John.

"Oh no—he did not come in," said Nellie. John continued to work in silence. At some distance from where he was, Mrs. Goddard was talking to Mrs. Ambrose. He could see her graceful figure, but he could hardly distinguish her features in the gloom of the dimly-lighted church. He longed to leave Nellie and to go and speak to her, but an undefined feeling of hurt pride prevented him. He would not forgive her for having taken the vicar's arm in coming home through the park; so he stayed where he was, pricking his fingers with the holly and rather impatiently pulling the string off the ball which Nellie held. If Mrs. Goddard wanted to speak to him, she might come of her own accord, he thought, for he felt that he had behaved foolishly in asking if she wished to see his odes. Somehow, when he thought about it, the odes did not seem so good now as they had seemed that afternoon.

Mrs. Goddard had not seen him at first, and for some time she remained in consultation with Mrs. Ambrose. At last she turned and looking for Nellie saw that she was seated beside John; to his great delight she came towards him. She looked more lovely than ever, he thought; the dark fur about her throat set off her delicate, sad face like a frame.

"Oh—are you here, too, Mr. Short?" she said.

"Hard at work, as you see," answered John. "Are you going to help, Mrs. Goddard? Won't you help me?"

"I wanted to," said Nellie, appealing to her mother, "but they would not let me, so I can only hold the string."

"Well, dear—we will see if we can help Mr. Short," said Mrs. Goddard good-naturedly, and she sat down upon the choir bench.

John never forgot that delightful Christmas Eve. For nearly two hours he never left Mrs.

Goddard's side, asking her advice about every branch and bit of holly and following out to the letter her most minute suggestions. He forgot all about the squire and about the walk back from the park, in the delight of having Mrs. Goddard to himself. He pushed the school-children about and spoke roughly to old Reynolds if her commands were not instantly executed; he felt in the little crowd of village people that he was her natural protector, and he wished he might never have anything in the world to do save to decorate a church in her company. He grew more and more confidential and when the work was all done he felt that he had thoroughly established himself in her good graces and went home to dream of the happiest day he had ever spent. The organ ceased playing, the little choir dispersed, the school children were sent home, Mr. Abraham Boosey retired to the bar of the Duke's Head, Muggins tenderly embraced every tombstone he met on his way through the churchyard, the " gentlefolk " followed Reynolds' lantern towards the vicarage, and Mr. Thomas Reid, the conservative and melancholic sexton, put out the lights and locked the church doors, muttering a sour laudation of more primitive times, when " the gentlefolk minded their business."

For the second time that day, John and Mr. Ambrose walked as far as the cottage, to see Mrs. Goddard to her home. When they parted from her and Nellie, John was careful not to say anything more about the odes, a subject to which Mrs. Goddard had not referred in the course of the evening. John thanked her rather effusively for her help—he could never have got through those choir benches without her, he said ; and the vicar added that he was very much obliged, too, and surreptitiously conveyed to Mrs. Goddard's hand a small package intended for Miss Nellie's Christmas stocking, from him and his wife, and which he had forgotten to give earlier. Nellie was destined to have a fuller stocking than usual this year, for the squire had remembered her as well as Mr. Ambrose.

John went to bed in his old room at the vicarage protesting that he had enjoyed the first day of his holiday immensely. As he blew

out the light, he thought suddenly how often
in that very room he had gone to bed dreaming
about the lady in black and composing verses
to her, till somehow the Greek terminations
would get mixed up with the Latin roots, the
quantities all seemed to change places, and he
used to fall asleep with a delicious half romantic
sense of happiness always unfulfilled yet always
present.   And now at last it began to be fulfilled
in earnest; he had met the lady in black at
last, had spent nearly half a day in her company
and was more persuaded than ever that she was
really and truly his ideal.   He did not go to sleep
so soon as in the old days, and he was sorry to
go to sleep at all; he wanted to enjoy all his
delicious recollections of that afternoon before
he slept and, as he recapitulated the events
which had befallen him and recalled each expression of the face that had charmed him and
every intonation of the charmer's voice, he felt
that he had never been really happy before,
that no amount of success at Cambridge could
give him half the delight he had experienced
during one hour in the old Billingsfield church,

and that altogether life anywhere else was not worth living. To-morrow he would see Mrs. Goddard again, and the next day and the day after that and then — "bother the future!" ejaculated John, and went to sleep.

He awoke early, roused by the loud clanging of the Christmas bells, and looking out he saw that the day was fine and cold and bright as Christmas day should be, and generally is. The hoar frost was frozen into fantastic shapes upon his little window, the snow was clinging to the yew branches outside and the robins were hopping and chirping over the thin crust of frozen snow that just covered the ground. The road was hard and brown as on the previous day, and the ice in the park would probably bear. Perhaps Mrs. Goddard would skate in the afternoon between the services, but then — Juxon would be there. "Never mind Juxon," quoth John to himself, "it is Christmas day!"

At the vicarage and elsewhere, all over the land, those things were done which delight the heart of Englishmen at the merry season. Everybody shook hands with everybody else, everybody cried "Merry Christmas!" to his neighbour in the street, with an intonation as though he were saying something startlingly new and brilliant which had never been said before. Every labourer who had a new smock-frock put it on, and those who had none had at least a bit of new red worsted comforter about their throats and began the day by standing at their doors in the cold morning, smoking a "ha'p'orth o' shag" in a new clay pipe, greeting each other across the village street. Muggins, who had spent a portion of the night in exchanging affectionate Christmas wishes with the tombstones in the churchyard, appeared fresh and ruddy at an early hour, clad in the long black coat and tall hat which he was accustomed to wear when he drove Mr. Boosey's fly on great festivals. Most of the cottages in the single street sported a bit of holly in their windows, and altogether the appearance of Billingsfield was singularly festive and mirthful. At precisely ten minutes to eleven the vicar and Mrs. Ambrose, accompanied by John, issued from the vicarage and went across the road by the private path

to the church. As they entered the porch Mr.
Reid, who stood solemnly tolling the small bell,
popularly nicknamed the "Ting-tang," and of
which the single rope passed down close to the
south door, vouchsafed John a sour smile of
recognition. John felt as though he had come
home.

Mrs. Goddard and Nellie appeared a moment
afterwards and took their seats in the pew
traditionally belonging to the cottage, behind
that of the squire who was always early, and the
sight of whose smoothly brushed hair and brown
beard was a constant source of satisfaction to
Mrs. Ambrose. John and Mrs. Ambrose sat
on the opposite side of the aisle, but John's
eyes strayed very frequently towards Mrs. Goddard; so frequently indeed that she noticed it
and leaned far back in her seat to avoid his
glance. Whereupon John blushed and felt that
the vicar, who was reading the Second Lesson,
had probably noticed his distraction. It was
hard to realise that two years and a half had
passed since he had sat in that same pew;
perhaps, however, the presence of Mrs. Goddard

helped him to understand the lapse of time. But for her it would have been very hard; for the vicar's voice sounded precisely as it used to sound; Mrs. Ambrose had not lost her habit of removing one glove and putting it into her prayer book as a mark while she found the hymn in the accompanying volume; the bright decorations looked as they looked years ago above the organ and round the chancel; from far down the church, just before the sermon, came the old accustomed sound of small boys shuffling their hobnailed shoes upon the stone floor and the audible guttural whisper of the church-warden admonishing them to "mind the stick;" the stained-glass windows admitted the same pleasant light as of yore—all was unchanged. But Mrs. Goddard and Nellie occupied the cottage pew, and their presence alone was suffi-cient to mark to John the fact that he was now a man.

The service was sympathetic to John Short. He liked the simplicity of it, even the rough singing of the choir, as compared with the solemn and magnificent musical services of Trinity College

Chapel. But it seemed very long before it was all over and he was waiting for Mrs. Goddard outside the church door.

There were more greetings, more "Merry Christmas" and "Many happy returns." Mrs. Goddard looked more charming than ever and was quite as cordial as on the previous evening.

"How much better it all looked this morning by daylight," she said.

"I think it looked very pretty last night," answered John. "There is nothing so delightful as Christmas decorations, is there?"

"Perhaps you will come down next year and help us again?" suggested Mrs. Goddard.

"Yes—well, I might come at Easter, for that matter," answered the young man, who after finding it impossible to visit Billingsfield during two years and a half, now saw no difficulty whatever in the way of making two visits in the course of six months. "Do you still decorate at Easter?" he asked.

"Oh yes—do you think you can come?" she said pleasantly. "I thought you were to be very busy just then."

"Yes, that is true," answered John. "But of course I could come, you know, if it were necessary."

"Hardly exactly necessary——" Mrs. Goddard laughed.

"The doctor told me some relaxation was absolutely indispensable for my health," said John rather sententiously.

"You don't really look very ill——are you?" She seemed incredulous.

"Oh no, of course not——only a little overworked sometimes."

"In that case I have no doubt it would do you good," said Mrs. Goddard.

"Do you really think so?" asked John, hopefully.

"Oh——that is a matter for your doctor to decide. I cannot possibly tell," she answered.

"I think you would make a very good doctor, Mrs. Goddard," said John venturing on a bolder flight.

"Really——I never thought of trying it," she replied with a little laugh. "Good morning Mr. Ambrose. Nellie wants to thank you for your beautiful present. It was really too good of you."

The vicar came out of the vestry and joined the group in the path. Mrs. Ambrose who had been asking Tom Judd's wife about her baby, also came up, and the squire, who had been presenting Mr. Reid with ten shillings for his Christmas box and who looked singularly bereaved without the faithful Stamboul at his heels, sauntered up and began congratulating everybody. In the distance the last of the congregation, chiefly the old women and cripples who could not keep up with the rest, hobbled away through the white gate of the churchyard.

It had been previously agreed that if the ice would bear there should be skating in the afternoon and the squire was anxious to inform the party that the pond was in excellent condition.

"As black as your hat," he said cheerfully. "Stamboul and I have been sliding all over it, so of course it would bear an ox. It did not crack anywhere."

"Do you skate, Mrs. Goddard?" asked John.

"Not very well — not nearly so well as Nellie.   But I am very fond of it."

"Will you let me push you about in a chair, then?   It is capital fun."

"Very good fun for me, no doubt," answered Mrs. Goddard, laughing.

"I would rather do it than anything else," said John in a tone of conviction.   "It is splendid exercise, pushing people about in chairs."

"So it is," said the squire, heartily.   "We will take turns, Mr. Short."   The suggestion did not meet with any enthusiastic response from John, who wished Mr. Juxon were not able to skate.

Poor John, he had but one idea, which consisted simply in getting Mrs. Goddard to himself as often and as long as possible. Unfortunately this idea did not coincide with Mr. Juxon's views.   Mr. Juxon was an older, slower and calmer man than the enthusiastic young scholar, and though very far from obtruding his views or making any assertion of his rights, was equally far from forgetting them. He was a man more of actions than words.   He had been in the habit of monopolising Mrs. Goddard's society for months and he had no intention of relinquishing his claims, even for the charitable purpose of allowing a poor student to enjoy his Christmas holiday and bit of romance undisturbed. If John had presented himself as a boy, it might have been different; but John emphatically considered himself a man, and the squire was quite willing to treat him as such, since he desired it. That is to say he would not permit him to "cut him out" as he would have expressed it. The result of the position in which John and Mr. Juxon soon found themselves was to be expected.

CHAPTER VIII.

JOHN did not sleep so peacefully nor dream so happily that night as on the night before. The course of true love had not run smooth that afternoon. The squire had insisted upon having his share of the lovely Mrs. Goddard's society and she herself had not seemed greatly disturbed at a temporary separation from John. The latter amused her for a little while; the former held the position of a friend whose conversation she liked better than that of other people. John was disappointed and thought of going back to Cambridge the next day. So strong, indeed was his sudden desire to leave Billingsfield without finishing his visit, that before going to bed he had packed some of his belongings into his small portmanteau; the tears almost stood in his eyes as he busied himself about his room and he muttered certain formulæ of self-accusation as he collected his things, saying over and over in his heart—"What a fool I am! Why should she care for me? What am I that she should care for me?" etc. etc. Then he opened his window and looked at the bright stars which shone out over the old yew tree; but it was exceedingly cold, and so he shut it again and went to bed, feeling very uncomfortable and unhappy.

But when he awoke in the morning he looked at his half-packed portmanteau and laughed, and instead of saying "What a fool I am!" he said "What a fool I was!"—which is generally and in most conditions of human affairs a much wiser thing to say. Then he carefully took everything out of the portmanteau again and replaced things as they had lain before in his room, lest perchance Susan, the housemaid, should detect what had passed through his mind on the previous evening and should tell Mrs. Ambrose. And from all this it appears that John was exceedingly young, as indeed he was, in spite of his being nearly one and twenty years of age. But doubtless if men were willing to confess their disappointments and foolish, impetuous resolutions, many would be found who have done likewise, being in years much older than John Short. Unfortunately for human nature most men would rather confess to positive wrong-doing than to any such youthful follies as these, while they are young; and when they are old they would rather be thought young and foolish than confess the evil deeds they have actually done.

John, however, did not moralise upon his situation. The weather was again fine and as he dressed his spirits rose. He became magnanimous and resolved to forget yesterday and make the most of to-day. He would see Mrs. Goddard of course; perhaps he would show her a little coldness at first, giving her to understand that she had not treated him well on the previous afternoon; then he would interest her by his talk—he would repeat to her one of those unlucky odes and translate it for her benefit, making use of the freedom he would thus get in order to make her an unlimited number of graceful compliments. Perhaps, too, he ought to pay more attention to Nellie, if he wished to conciliate her mother. Women, he reflected, have such strange prejudices !

He wondered whether it would be proper for him to call upon Mrs. Goddard. He was not quite sure about it, and he was rather ashamed of having so little knowledge of the world; but he believed that in Billingsfield he might run the risk. There had been talk of skating again that morning, and so, about ten o'clock, John told Mr. Ambrose he would go for a short walk and then join them all at the pond in the park. The project seemed good, and he put it into execution. As he walked up the frozen road, he industriously repeated in his mind the Greek verses he was going to translate to Mrs. Goddard; he had no copy of them but his memory was very good. He met half a dozen labourers, strolling about with their pipes until it was time to go and have a pint of beer, as is their manner upon holidays; they touched their hats to him, remembering his face well, and he smiled happily at the rough fellows, contrasting his situation with theirs, who from the misfortune of social prejudice were not permitted to go and call upon Mrs. Goddard.

His heart beat rather fast as he went up to the door of the cottage, and for one unpleasant moment he again doubted whether it was proper for him to make such an early visit.   But being bent on romantic adventure he rang boldly and inquired for Mrs. Goddard.

She was surprised to see John at that hour and alone; but it did not enter her head to refuse him admittance.   Indeed as he stood in the little passage he heard the words which passed between her and Martha.

"What is it, Martha?"

"It's a young gentleman mam.   I rather think, mam, it's the young gentleman that's stopping at the vicarage."

"Oh—ask him to come in."

"In 'ere mam?"

"No—into the sitting-room," said Mrs. Goddard, who was busy in the dining-room.

John was accordingly ushered in and told to wait a minute; which he did, surveying with surprise the beautiful pictures, the rich looking furniture and the valuable objects that lay about upon the tables.   He experienced a thrill of pleasure, for he felt sure that Mrs. Goddard possessed another qualification which he had unconsciously attributed to her—that of being accustomed to a certain kind of luxury, which in John's mind was mysteriously connected with his romance. It is one of the most undefinable of the many indefinite feelings to which young men in love are subject, especially young men who have been, or are, very poor. They like to connect ideas of wealth and comfort, even of a luxurious existence, with the object of their affections. They desire the world of love to be new to them, and in order to be wholly new in their experience, it must be rich. The feeling is not so wholly unworthy as it might seem; they instinctively place their love upon a pedestal and require its surroundings to be of a better kind than such as they have been accustomed to in their own lives. King Cophetua, being a king, could afford to love the beggar maid, and a very old song sings of a "lady who loved a swine," but the names of the poor young men who have loved above their fortune and station are innumerable as the swallows in spring. John saw that Mrs. Goddard was much richer than he had ever been, and without the smallest second thought was pleased.   In a few moments she entered the room.   John had his speech ready.

"I thought, if you were going to skate, I would call and ask leave to go with you," he said glibly, as she gave him her hand.

"Oh—thanks.   But is not it rather early?"

"It is twenty minutes past ten," said John looking at the clock.

"Well, let us get warm before starting," said Mrs. Goddard, sitting down by the fire.   "It is so cold this morning."

John thought she was lovely to look at as she sat there, warming her hands and shielding her face from the flame with them at the same time. She looked at him and smiled pleasantly, but said nothing.   She was still a little surprised to see him and wondered whether he himself had anything to say.

"Yes," said John, "it is very cold—traditional Christmas weather.   Could not be finer, in fact, could it?"

"No—it could not be finer," echoed Mrs.

Goddard, suppressing a smile. Then as though to help him out of his embarrassment by giving an impulse to the conversation, she added, " By the bye, Mr. Short, while we are warming ourselves why do not you let me hear one of your odes ? "

She meant it kindly, thinking it would give him pleasure, as indeed it did. John's heart leaped and he blushed all over his face with delight. Mrs. Goddard was not quite sure whether she had done right, but she attributed his evident satisfaction to his vanity as a scholar.

" Certainly," he said with alacrity, " if you would like to hear it. Would you care to hear me repeat the Greek first ? "

" Oh, of all things. I do not think I have ever heard Greek."

John cleared his throat and began, glancing at his hostess rather nervously from time to time. But his memory never failed him, and he went on to the end without a break or hesitation.

" How do you think it sounds ? " he asked timidly when he had finished.

" It sounds very funny," said Mrs. Goddard.

"I had no idea Greek sounded like that—but it has a pleasant rhythm."

"That is the thing," said John, enthusiastically. "I see you really appreciate it. Of course nobody knows how the ancients pronounced Greek, and if one pronounced it as the moderns do, it would sound all wrong—but the rhythm is the thing, you know. It is impossible to get over that."

Mrs. Goddard was not positively sure what he meant by "getting over the rhythm;" possibly John himself could not have defined his meaning very clearly. But his cheeks glowed and he was very much pleased.

"Yes, of course," said Mrs. Goddard confidently. "But what does it all mean, Mr. Short?"

"Would you really like to know?" asked John in fresh embarrassment. He suddenly realised how wonderfully delightful it was to be repeating his own poetry to the woman for whom it was written.

"Indeed yes—what is the use of your telling me all sorts of things in Greek, if you do not tell me what they mean?"

"Yes—you will promise not to be offended?"

“Of course,” said Mrs. Goddard; then blushing a little she added, “it is quite—I mean—quite the sort of thing, is not it?”

“Oh quite,” said John, blushing too, but looking grave for a moment. Then he repeated the English translation of the verses which, as they were certainly not so good as the original, may be omitted here. They set forth that in the vault of the world’s night a new star had appeared which men had not yet named, nor would be likely to name until the power of human speech should be considerably increased, and the verses dwelt upon the theme, turning it and revolving it in several ways, finally declaring that the far-darting sun must look out for his interests unless he meant to be outshone by the new star. Translated into English there was nothing very remarkable about the performance though the original Greek ode was undoubtedly very good of its kind. But Mrs. Goddard was determined to be pleased.

“I think it is charming,” she said, when John had reached the end and paused for her criticism.

“The Greek is very much better,” said John

doubtfully. "I cannot write English verses—
they seem to me so much harder."

"I daresay," said Mrs. Goddard. "But did
you really write that when—" she stopped not
knowing exactly how to express herself. But
John had his answer ready.

"Oh, I wrote ever so many," he said, "and I
have got them all at Cambridge. But that is the
only one I quite remember. I wrote them just
after the day when I waked up Muggins—the
only time I had seen you till now. I think I
could——"

"How funny it seems," said Mrs. Goddard,
"without knowing a person, to write verses to
them! How did you manage to do it?"

"I was going to say that I think—I am quite sure
—I could write much better things to you now."

"Oh, that is impossible—quite absurd, Mr.
Short," said Mrs. Goddard, laughing more gaily
than usual.

"Why?" asked John, somewhat emboldened
by his success. "I do not see why, if one has
an ideal, you know, one should not understand
it much better when one comes near to it."

“Yes—but—how can I possibly be your ideal?” She felt herself so much older than John that she thought it was out of the question to be annoyed; so she treated him in a matter of fact way, and was really amused at his talk.

“I don’t see why not,” answered John stoutly. “You might be any man’s ideal.”

“Oh, really—” ejaculated Mrs. Goddard, somewhat startled at the force of the sweeping compliment. To be told point-blank, even by an enthusiastic youth of one and twenty, that one is the ideal woman, must be either very pleasant or very startling.

“Excuse me,” she said quickly, before he could answer her, “you know of course I am very ignorant—yes I am—but will you please tell me what is an ‘ideal’?”

“Why—yes,” said John, “it is very easy. Ideal comes from idea. Plato meant, by the idea, the perfect model—well, do you see?”

“Not exactly,” said Mrs. Goddard.

“It is very simple. When I, when anybody, says you are the ideal woman, it is meant that you are the perfect model, the archetype of a woman."

"Yes—but that is absurd," said his companion rather coldly.

"I am sorry that it should seem absurd," said John in a persuasive tone; "it seems very natural to me. A man thinks for a long time about everything that most attracts him and then, on a sudden, he sees it all before him, quite real and alive, and then he says he has realised his ideal. But you liked the verses, Mrs. Goddard?" he added quickly, hoping to bring back the smile that had vanished from her face. He had a strong impression that he had been a little too familiar. Probably Mrs. Goddard thought so too.

"Oh yes, I think they are very nice," she answered. But the smile did not come back. She was not displeased, but she was not pleased either; she was wondering how far this boy would go if she would let him. John, however, felt unpleasantly doubtful about what he had done.

"I hope you are not displeased," he said.

“Oh, not in the least,” said she. “Shall we go to the park and skate?”

“I am not sure that I will skate to-day,” said John, foolishly. Mrs. Goddard looked at him in unfeigned surprise.

“Why not? I thought it was for that——”

“Oh, of course,” said John quickly. “Only it is not very amusing to skate when Mr. Juxon is pushing you about in a chair.”

“Really—why should not he push me about, if I like it?”

“If you like it—that is different,” answered John impatiently.

Mrs. Goddard began to think that John was very like a spoiled child, and she resented his evident wish to monopolise her society. She left the room to get ready for the walk, vaguely wishing that he had not come.

“I have made a fool of myself again,” said John to himself, when he was left alone; and he suddenly wished he could get out of the house without seeing her again. But before he had done wishing, she returned.

“Where is Miss Nellie?” he asked gloomily,

as they walked down the path. " I hope she is coming too."

"She went up to the pond with Mr. Juxon, just before you came."

" Do you let her go about like that, without you ?" asked John severely.

" Why not?   Really, Mr. Short," said Mrs. Goddard, glancing up at his face, " either you dislike Mr. Juxon very much, or else I think you take a good deal upon yourself in remarking —in this way——"

She was naturally a little timid, but John's youth and what she considered as his extraordinary presumption inspired her with courage to protest.   The effect upon John was instantaneous.

" Pray forgive me," he said humbly, " I am very silly.   I daresay you are quite right and I do not like Mr. Juxon.   Not that I have the smallest reason for not liking him," he continued quickly, " it is a mere personal antipathy, a mere idea, I daresay——very foolish of me."

" It is very foolish to take unreasonable dislikes to people one knows nothing about," she said quietly.   "Will you please open the gate ?"

They were standing before the bars, but John was so much disturbed in mind that he stood still, quite forgetting to raise the long iron latch.

"Dear me—I beg your pardon—I cannot imagine what I was thinking of," he said making the most idiotic excuse current in English idiom.

"Nor I," said Mrs. Goddard, with a little laugh, as he held the gate back for her to pass. It was a plain white gate with stone pillars, and there was no gate-house. People who came to the Hall were expected to open it for themselves. Mrs. Goddard was so much amused at John's absence of mind that her good humour returned, and he felt that since that object was attained he no longer regretted his folly in the least. The cloud that had darkened the horizon of his romance had passed quickly away, and once more he said inwardly that he was enjoying the happiest days of his life. If for a moment the image of Mr. Juxon entered the field of his imaginative vision in the act of pushing Mrs. Goddard's chair upon the ice, he mentally ejaculated "bother the squire!" as he had done upon the previous night, and soon forgot all about him. The way through the park · was long, the morning was delightful and Mrs. Goddard did not seem to be in a hurry.

"I wish the winter would last for ever," he said presently.

"So do I," answered his companion, "it is the pleasantest time of the year. One does not feel that nature is dead because one is sure she will very soon be alive again."

"That is a charming idea," said John, "one might make a good subject of it."

"It is a little old, perhaps. I think I have heard it before—have not you?"

"All good ideas are old. The older the better," said John confidently. Mrs. Goddard could not resist the temptation of teazing him a little. They had grown very intimate in forty-eight hours; it had taken six months for Mr. Juxon to reach the point John had won in two days.

"Are they?" she asked quietly. "Is that the reason you selected me for the 'idea' of your ode, which you explained to me?"

"You?" said John in astonishment. Then

he laughed. "Why, you are not any older than I am!"

"Do you think so?" she inquired with a demure smile. "I am very much older than you think."

"You must be—I mean, you know, you must be older than you look."

"Thank you," said Mrs. Goddard, still smiling, and just resting the tips of her fingers upon his arm as she stepped across a slippery place in the frozen road. "Yes, I am a great deal older than you."

John would have liked very much to ask her age, but even to his youthful and unsophisticated mind such a question seemed almost too personal. He did not really believe that she was more than five years older than he, and that seemed to be no difference at all.

"I don't know," he said. "I am nearly one and twenty."

"Yes, I know," said Mrs. Goddard, who had heard every detail concerning John from Mr. Ambrose, again and again. "Just think," she added with a laugh, "only one and twenty!

Why when I was one and twenty I was——" she stopped short.

"What were you doing then?" asked John, trying not to seem too curious.

"I was living in London," she said quietly. She half enjoyed his disappointment.

"Yes," he said, "I daresay. But what—well, I suppose I ought not to ask any questions."

"Certainly not," said she. "It is very rude to ask a lady questions about her age."

"I do not mean to be rude again," said John, pretending to laugh. "Have you always been fond of skating?" he asked, fixing his eye upon a distant tree, and trying to look unconscious.

"No—I only learned since I came here. Besides, I skate very badly."

"Did Mr. Juxon teach you?" asked John, still gazing into the distance. From not looking at the path he slipped on a frozen puddle and nearly fell. Whereat, as usual, when he did anything awkward, he blushed to the brim of his hat.

"Take care," said Mrs. Goddard, calmly. "You will fall if you don't look where you are going.   No; Mr. Juxon was not here last year. He only came here in the summer."

"It seems to me that he has always been here," said John, trying to recover his equanimity. "Then I suppose Mr. Ambrose taught you to skate?"

"Exactly—Mr. Ambrose taught me.   He skates very well."

"So will you, with a little more practice,' answered her companion in a rather patronising tone.   He intended perhaps to convey the idea that Mrs. Goddard would improve in the exercise if she would actually skate, and with him, instead of submitting to be pushed about in a chair by Mr. Juxon.

"Oh, I daresay," said Mrs. Goddard indifferently. "We shall soon be there, now.   I can hear them on the ice."

"Too soon," said John with regret.

"I thought you liked skating so much."

"I like walking with you much better," he replied, and he glanced at her face to see if his speech produced any sign of sympathy.

"You have walked with me; now you can skate with Nellie," suggested Mrs. Goddard.

"You talk as though I were a child," said John, suddenly losing his temper in a very unaccountable way.

"Because I said you might skate with Nellie? Really, I don't see why. Mr. Juxon is not a child, and he has been skating with her all the morning."

"That is different," retorted John growing very red.

"Yes—Nellie is much nearer to your age than to Mr. Juxon's," answered Mrs. Goddard, with a calmness which made John desperate.

"Really, Mrs. Goddard," he said stiffly, "I cannot see what that has to do with it."

"'The atrocious crime of being a young man, which the lady so much older than myself has charged—' How does the quotation end, Mr Short?"

"'Has, with such spirit and decency, charged upon me, I shall neither attempt to palliate nor deny,'" said John savagely. "Quite so, Mrs. Goddard. I shall not attempt to palliate it, nor will I venture to deny it."

"Then why in the world are you so angry

with me?" she asked, suddenly turning her violet eyes upon him. "I was only laughing, you know."

"Only laughing!" repeated John. "It is more pleasant to laugh than to be laughed at."

"Yes—would not you allow me the pleasure then, just for once?"

"Certainly, if you desire it. You are so extremely merry——"

"Come, Mr. Short, we must not seem to have been quarrelling when we reach the pond. It would be too ridiculous."

"Everything seems to strike you in a humorous light to-day," answered John, beginning to be pacified by her tone.

"Do you know, you are much more interesting when you are angry," said Mrs. Goddard.

"And you only made me angry in order to see whether I was interesting?"

"Perhaps—but then, I could not help it in the least."

"I trust you are thoroughly satisfied upon the point, Mrs. Goddard? If there is anything more that I can do to facilitate your researches in psychology——"

"You would help me?   Even to the extent of being angry again?"   She smiled so pleasantly and frankly that John's wrath vanished.

"It is impossible to be angry with you.   I am very sorry if I seemed to be," he answered.   "A man who has the good fortune to be thrown into your society is a fool to waste his time in being disagreeable."

"I agree with the conclusion, at all events— that is, it is much better to be agreeable.   Is it not?   Let us be friends."

"Oh, by all means," said John.

They walked on for some minutes in silence. John reflected that he had witnessed a phase of Mrs. Goddard's character of which he had been very far from suspecting the existence.   He had not hitherto imagined her to be a woman of quick temper or sharp speech.   His idea of her was formed chiefly upon her appearance.   Her sad face, with its pathetic expression, suggested a melancholy humour delighting in subdued and tranquil thoughts, inclined naturally to the romantic view, or to what in the eyes of youths of twenty appears to be the romantic view of life. He had suddenly found her answering him with a sharpness which, while it roused his wits, startled his sensibilities. . But he was flattered as well. His instinct and his observation of Mrs. Goddard when in the society of others led him to believe that with Mr. and Mrs. Ambrose, or even with Mr. Juxon, she was not in the habit of talking as she talked with him. He was therefore inwardly pleased, so soon as his passing annoyance had subsided, to feel that she made a difference between him and others.

It was quite true that she made a distinction, though she did so almost unconsciously. It was perfectly natural, too. She was young in heart in spite of her thirty years and her troubles, she had an elastic temperament; to a physiognomist her face would have shown a delicate sensitiveness to impressions rather than any inborn tendency to sadness. In spite of everything she was still young, and for two years and a half she had been in the society of persons much older than herself, persons she respected and regarded as friends, but persons in whom her youth found no sympathy. It was natural, therefore, that when time to some extent had healed the wound she had suffered and she suddenly found herself in the society of a young and enthusiastic man, something of the enforced soberness of her manner should unbend, showing her character in a new light. She herself enjoyed the change, hardly knowing why; she enjoyed a little passage of arms with John, and it amused her more than she could have expected to be young again, to annoy him, to break the peace and heal it again in five minutes. But what happened entirely failed to amuse the squire, who did not regard such diversions as harmless; and moreover she was far from expecting the effect which her treatment of John Short produced upon his scholarly but enthusiastic temper.

CHAPTER IX.

THE squire had remarked that John Short seemed
to have a peculiar temper, and Mrs. Goddard had
observed the same thing. What has gone before
sufficiently explains the change in John's manner,
and the difference in his behaviour was plainly
apparent even to Mr. and Mrs. Ambrose. The
vicar indeed was wise enough to see that John
was very much attracted by Mrs. Goddard, but
he was also wise enough to say nothing about
it. His wife, however, who had witnessed no love-
making for nearly thirty years, except the court-
ship of the young physician who had married
her daughter, attributed John's demeanour to no
such disturbing cause. He was overworked, she
said; he was therefore irritable; he had of course
never taken that excellent homœopathic remedy,
highly diluted aconite, since he had left the

vicarage; the consequence was that he was subject to nervous headache—she only hoped he would not be taken ill on the eve of the examination for honours. She hoped, too, that he would prolong his holiday to the very last moment, for the country air and the rest he enjoyed were sure to do him so much good. With regard to the extension of John's visit, the vicar thought differently, although he held his peace. There were many reasons why John should not become attached to Mrs. Goddard both for her sake and his own, and if he staid long, the vicar felt quite sure that he would fall in love with her. She was dangerously pretty, she was much older than John—which in the case of very young men constitutes an additional probability—she evidently took an innocent pleasure in his society, and altogether such a complication as was likely to ensue was highly undesirable. Therefore, when Mrs. Ambrose pressed John to stay longer than he had intended, the vicar not only gave him no encouragement, but spoke gravely of the near approach of the contest for honours, of the necessity of concentrating every force for the coming struggle, and expressed at the same time the firm conviction that, if John did his best, he ought to be the senior classic in the year.

Even Mrs. Goddard urged him to go. Of course he asked her advice. He would not have lost that opportunity of making her speak of himself, nor of gauging the exact extent of the interest he hoped she felt in him.

It was two or three days after the long conversation he had enjoyed with her. In that time they had met often and John's admiration for her, strengthened by his own romantic desire to be really in love, had begun to assume proportions which startled Mrs. Goddard and annoyed Mr. Juxon. The latter felt that the boy was in his way; whenever he wanted to see Mrs. Goddard, John was at her side, talking eagerly and contesting his position against the squire with a fierceness which in an older and wiser man would have been in the worst possible taste. Even as it was, Mr. Juxon looked considerably annoyed as he stood by, smoothing his smooth hair from time to time with his large white hand

and feeling that even at his age, and with his experience, a man might sometimes cut a poor figure.

On the particular occasion when the relations between John and the squire became an object of comment to Mrs. Ambrose, the whole party were assembled at Mrs. Goddard's cottage. She had invited everybody to tea, a meal which in her little household represented a compromise between her appetite and Nellie's. She had felt that in the small festivities of the Billingsfield Christmas season she was called upon to do her share with the rest and, being a simple woman, she took her part simply, and did not dignify the entertainment of her four friends by calling it a dinner. The occasion was none the less hospitable, for she gave both time and thought to her preparations. Especially she had considered the question of precedence; it was doubtful, she thought, whether the squire or the vicar should sit upon her right hand. The squire, as being lord of the manor, represented the powers temporal, the vicar on the other hand represented the church, which on ordinary occasions takes precedence of the lay faculty. She had at last privately consulted Mr. Juxon, in whom she had the greatest confidence, asking him frankly which she should do, and Mr. Juxon had unhesitatingly yielded the post of honour to the vicar, adding to enforce his opinion the very plausible argument that if he, the squire, took Mrs. Goddard in to tea, the vicar would have to give his arm either to little Nellie or to his own wife. Mrs. Goddard was convinced and the affair was a complete success.

John felt that he could not complain of his position, but as he was separated from the object of his admiration during the whole meal, he resolved to indemnify himself for his sufferings by monopolising her conversation during the rest of the evening. The squire on the other hand, who had been obliged to talk to Mrs. Ambrose during most of the time while they were at table, and who, moreover, was beginning to feel that he had seen almost enough of John Short, determined to give the young man a lesson in the art of interesting women in general and Mrs. Goddard in particular. She, indeed, would

not have been a woman at all had she not
understood the two men and their intentions.
After tea the party congregated round the fire in
the little drawing-room, standing in a circle, of
which their hostess formed the centre.   Mr.
Juxon and John, anticipating that Mrs. Goddard
must ultimately sit upon one side or other of
the fireplace had at first chosen opposite sides,
each hoping that she would take the chair nearest
to himself.   But Mrs. Goddard remained standing
an unreasonably long time, for the very reason
that she did not choose to sit beside either of
them.   Seeing this the squire, who had perhaps
a greater experience than his adversary in this
kind of strategic warfare, left his place and put
himself on he same side as John.   He argued
that Mrs. Goddard would probably then choose
the opposite side whereas John who was younger
would think she would come towards the two
where they stood ; John would consequently lose
time, Mr. Juxon would cross again and instal
himself by her side while his enemy was
hesitating.

While these moves and counter-moves were

proceeding, the conversation was general. The vicar was for the hundredth time admiring the Andrea del Sarto over the chimney-piece and his wife was explaining her general objections to the representation of sacred subjects upon canvas, while Mrs. Goddard answered each in turn and endeavoured to disagree with neither. What the squire had foreseen when he made his last move, however, actually took place at last. Mrs. Goddard established herself upon the side opposite the two men. Mr. Juxon crossed rapidly to where she was seated, and Mrs. Ambrose, who had turned with the intention of speaking to the squire, found herself confronted by John. He saw that he had been worsted by his foe and immediately lost his temper; but being brought face to face with Mrs. Ambrose was obliged to control it as he might. That excellent lady beamed upon him with a maternal smile of the kind which is peculiarly irritating to young men. He struggled to get away however, glancing over Mrs. Ambrose's shoulder at the squire and longing to be "at him" as he would have expressed it. But the squire was not to be got at so easily, for the vicar's wife was of a fine presence and covered much ground.   John involuntarily thought of the dyke before Troy, of Hector and his heroes attempting to storm it and of the Ajaces and Sarpedon defending it and glaring down from above.   He could appreciate Hector's feelings—Mrs. Ambrose was very like the dyke.

The squire smiled serenely and smoothed his hair as he talked to Mrs. Goddard and she herself looked by no means discontented, thereby adding, as it were, an insult to the injury done to John.

"I shall always envy you the cottage," the squire was saying.   "I have not a single room in the Hall that is half so cheery in the evening."

"I shall never forget my terror when we first met," answered Mrs. Goddard, "do you remember?   You frightened me by saying you would like to live here.   I thought you meant it."

"You must have thought I was .the most unmannerly of barbarians."

"Instead of being the best of landlords," added Mrs. Goddard with a grateful smile.

"I hardly know whether I am that," said Mr. Juxon, settling himself in his chair. "But I believe I am by nature an exceedingly comfortable man, and I never fail to consult the interests of my comfort."

"And of mine. Think of all you have done to improve this place. I can never thank you enough. I suppose one always feels particularly grateful at Christmas time—does not one?"

"One has more to be grateful for, it seems to me—in our climate, too. People in southern countries never really know what comfort means, because nature never makes them thoroughly uncomfortable. Only a man who is freezing can appreciate a good fire."

"I suppose you have been a good deal in such places," suggested Mrs. Goddard, vaguely.

"Oh yes—everywhere," answered the squire with equal indefiniteness. "By the bye, talking of travelling, when is our young friend going away?" There was not a shade of ill-humour in the question.

"The day after New Year's—I believe."

"He has had a very pleasant visit."

"Yes," replied Mrs. Goddard, "I hope it will do him a great deal of good."

"Why? Was he ill? Ah—I remember, they said he had worked too hard. It is a great mistake to work too hard, especially when one is very young."

"He is very young, is not he?" remarked Mrs. Goddard with a faint smile, remembering the many conversations she had had with him.

"Very. Did it ever strike you that—well, that he was losing his head a little?"

"No," answered his companion innocently. "What about?"

"Oh, nothing. Only he has rather a peculiar temper. He is perpetually getting very angry with no ostensible reason—and then he glares at one like an angry cat."

"Take care," said Mrs. Goddard, "he might hear you."

"Do him good," said the squire cheerfully.

"Oh, no! It would hurt his feelings dreadfully. How can you be so unkind?"

"He is a very good boy, you know. Really, I believe he is. Only he is inclined to be rather too unreasonable; I should think he might be satisfied."

"Satisfied with what?" inquired Mrs. Goddard, who did not wish to understand.

"With the way you have treated him," returned the squire bluntly. "You have been wonderfully good to him."

"Have I?" The faint colour rose to her cheek. "I don't know—poor fellow! I daresay his life at Cambridge is very dull."

"Yes. Entirely devoid of that species of amusement which he has enjoyed so abundantly in Billingsfield. It is not every undergraduate who has a chance to talk to you for a week at a time.'

Mr. Juxon made the remark very calmly, without seeming to be in the least annoyed. He was much too wise a man to appear to be displeased at Mrs. Goddard's treatment of John Moreover, he felt that on the present occasion, at least, John had been summarily worsted; it was his turn to be magnanimous.

"If you are going to make compliments, I will go away," said Mrs. Goddard.

"I ? I never made a compliment in my life," replied the squire complacently. "Do you think it is a compliment to tell you that Mr. Short probably enjoys your conversation much more than the study of Greek roots ? "

"Well—not exactly——"

"Besides, in general," continued the squire, "compliments are mere waste of breath. If a woman has any vanity she knows her own good points much better than any man who attempts to explain them to her; and if she has no vanity, no amount of explanation of her merits will make her see them in a proper light."

"That is very true," answered Mrs. Goddard thoughtfully. "It never struck me before. I wonder whether that is the reason women always like men who never make any compliments at all ?"

The squire's face assumed an amusing expression of inquiry and surprise.

" Is that personal ?" he asked.

"Oh—of course not," answered Mrs. Goddard

in some confusion. She blushed and turning towards the fire took up the poker and pretended to stir the coals. Women always delight in knocking a good fire to pieces, out of pure absence of mind. John Short saw the movement and, escaping suddenly from the maternal conversation of Mrs. Ambrose, threw himself upon his knee on the hearth-rug and tried to take the poker from his hostess's hand.

"Oh, Mrs. Goddard, don't! Let me do it—please!" he exclaimed.

"But I can do it very well myself," said she, protesting and not relaxing her hold upon the poker. But John was obstinate in his determination to save her trouble, and rudely tried to get the instrument away.

"Please don't—you hurt me," said Mrs. Goddard petulantly.

"Oh—I beg your pardon—I wanted to help you," said John leaving his hold. "I did not really hurt you—did I?" he asked, almost tenderly.

"Dreadfully," replied Mrs. Goddard, half angry and half amused at his impatience and subsequent contrition. The squire sat complacently in his chair, watching the little scene. John hated him more than ever, and grew very red. Mrs. Goddard saw the boy's embarrassment and presently relented.

"I daresay you will do it better than I," she said, handing him the poker, which John seized with alacrity. "That big coal—there," she added, pointing to a smouldering block in the corner of the grate.

"I did not mean to be rude," said John. "I only wanted to help you." He knelt by her side poking the fire industriously. "I only wanted to get a chance to talk to you," he added, in a low voice, barely audible to Mrs. Goddard as she leaned forward.

"I am afraid you cannot do that just now," she said, not unkindly, but with the least shade of severity in her tone. "You will get dreadfully hot if you stay there, so near the fire."

"I don't mind the heat in the least," said John heroically. Nevertheless as she did not give him any further encouragement he was presently obliged to retire, greatly discomfited.

He could not spend the evening on his knees with the poker in his hand.

"Bad failure," remarked the squire in an undertone as soon as John had rejoined Mrs. Ambrose, who had not quite finished her lecture on homœopathy.

Mrs. Goddard leaned back in her chair and looked at Mr. Juxon rather coolly. She did not want him to laugh at John, though she was not willing to encourage John herself.

"You should not be unkind," she said. "He is such a nice boy—why should you wish him to be uncomfortable."

"Oh, I don't in the least. I could not help being amused a little. I am sure I don't want to be unkind."

Indeed the squire had not shown himself to be so, on the whole, and he did not refer to the matter again during the evening. He kept his place for some time by Mrs. Goddard's side and then, judging that he had sufficiently asserted his superiority, rose and talked to Mrs. Ambrose. But John, being now in a thoroughly bad humour, could not take his vacant seat with a good grace. He stood aloof and took up a book that lay upon the table and avoided looking at Mrs. Goddard. By and by, when the party broke up, he said good-night in such a particularly cold and formal tone of voice that she stared at him in surprise. But he took no notice of her look and went away after the Ambroses, in that state of mind which boys call a huff.

But on the following day John repented of his behaviour. All day long he wandered about the garden of the vicarage, excusing himself from joining the daily skating which formed the staple of amusement during the Christmas week, by saying that he had an idea for a copy of verses and must needs work it out. But he inwardly hoped that Mrs. Goddard would come to the vicarage late in the afternoon, without the inevitable Mr. Juxon, and that he might then get a chance of talking to her. He was not quite sure what he should say. He would find words on the spur of the moment; it would at all events be much easier than to meet her on the ice at the Hall with all the rest of them and to see Mr. Juxon pushing her about in that detestable chair, with the unruffled air of superiority which John so hated to see upon his face. The vicar suspected more than ever that there was something wrong; he had seen some of the by-play on the previous evening, and had noticed John's ill-concealed disappointment at being unable to dislodge the sturdy squire from his seat. But Mrs. Ambrose seemed to be very obtuse, and the vicar would have been the last to have spoken of his suspicions, even to the wife of his bosom. It was his duty to induce John to go back to his work at the end of the week; it was not his duty to put imputations upon him which Mrs. Ambrose would naturally exaggerate and which would drive her excellent heart into a terrible state of nervous anxiety.

But Mrs. Goddard did not come back to the vicarage on that day, and John went to dinner with a sad heart. It did not seem like a day at all if he had not seen her and talked with her. He had now no doubt whatever that he was seriously in love, and he set himself to consider his position. The more he considered it, the more irreconcilable it seemed to be with the passion which beset him. A child could see that for several years, at least, he would not be in a position to marry. With Mr. Juxon at hand from year's end to year's end, the owner of the Hall, of the Billingsfield property and according to all appearances of other resources besides,—with such a man constantly devoted to her, could Mrs. Goddard be expected to wait for poor John three years, even two years, from the time of the examination for the classical Tripos ? Nothing was more improbable, he was forced to admit. And yet, the idea of life if he did not marry Mrs. Goddard was dismal beyond all expression; he would probably not survive it. He did not know what he should do. He shrank from the thought of declaring his love to her at once. He remembered with pain that she had a terrible way of laughing at him when he grew confidential or too complimentary, and he dreaded lest at the supreme moment of his life he should appear ridiculous in her eyes—he, a mere undergraduate. If he came out at the head of the Tripos it would be different; and yet that seemed so long to wait, especially while

Mr. Juxon lived at the Hall and Mrs. Goddard lived at the park gates. Suddenly a thought struck him which filled him with delight; it was just possible that Mr. Juxon had no intention of marrying Mrs. Goddard. If he had any such views he would probably have declared them before now, for he had met her every day during more than half a year. John longed to ask some one the question. Perhaps Mr. Ambrose, who might be supposed to know everything connected with Mrs. Goddard, could tell him. He felt very nervous at the idea of speaking to the vicar on the subject, and yet it seemed to him that no one else could set his mind at rest. If he were quite certain that Mr. Juxon had no intention of offering himself to the charming tenant of the cottage, he might return to his work with some sense of security in the future. Otherwise he saw only the desperate alternative of throwing himself at her feet and declaring that he loved her, or of going back to Cambridge with the dreadful anticipation of hearing any day that she had married the squire. To be laughed at would be bad, but to feel that he had lost her irrevocably, without a struggle, would be awful. No one but the vicar could and would tell him the truth; it would be bitter to ask such a question, but it must be done. Having at last come to this formidable resolution, towards the conclusion of dinner, his spirits rose a little. He took another glass of the vicar's mild ale and felt that he could face his fate.

"May I speak to you a moment in the study, Mr. Ambrose?" he said as they rose from table.

"Certainly," replied the vicar; and having conducted his wife to the drawing-room, he returned to find John. There was a low, smouldering fire in the study grate, and John had lit a solitary candle. The room looked very dark and dismal and John was seated in one of the black leather chairs, waiting.

"Anything about those verses you were speaking of to-day?" asked the vicar cheerfully, in anticipation of a pleasant classical chat.

"No," said John, gloomily. "The fact is—" he cleared his throat, "the fact is, I want to ask you rather a delicate question, sir."

The vicar's heavy eyebrows contracted; the lines of his face all turned downwards, and his long, clean-shaved upper lip closed sharply upon its fellow, like a steel trap. He turned his gray eyes upon John's averted face with a searching look.

"Have you got into any trouble at Trinity, John?" he asked severely.

"Oh no—no indeed," said John. Nothing was further from his thoughts than his college at that moment. "I want to ask you a question, which no one else can answer. Is—do you think that—that Mr. Juxon has any idea of marrying Mrs. Goddard?"

The vicar started in astonishment and laid both hands upon the arms of his chair.

"What—in the world—put that—into your head?" he asked very slowly, emphasising every word of his question. John was prepared to see his old tutor astonished but was rather taken aback at the vicar's tone.

"Do you think it is likely, sir?" he insisted.

"Certainly not," answered the vicar, still eyeing him suspiciously. "Certainly not. I have positive reasons to prove the contrary. But, my dear John, why, in the name of all that is sensible, do you ask me such a question?

You don't seriously think of proposing——"

"I don't see why I should not," said John doggedly, seeing that he was found out.

"You don't see why you should not? Why the thing is perfectly absurd, not to say utterly impossible! John, you are certainly mad."

"I don't see why," repeated John. "I am a grown man. I have good prospects——"

"Good prospects!" ejaculated the vicar in horror. "Good prospects! Why, you are only an undergraduate at Cambridge."

"I may be senior classic in a few months," objected John. "That is not such a bad prospect, it seems to me."

"It means that you may get a fellowship, probably will—in the course of a few years. But you lose it if you marry. Besides—do you know that Mrs. Goddard is ten years older than you, and more?"

"Impossible," said John in a tone of conviction.

"I know that she is. She will be two and

thirty on her next birthday, and you are not yet one and twenty."

"I shall be next month," argued John, who was somewhat taken aback, however, by the alarming news of Mrs. Goddard's age. "Besides, I can go into the church, before I get a fellowship——"

"No, you can't," said the vicar energetically. "You won't be able to manage it. If you do, you will have to put up with a poor living."

"That would not matter. Mrs. Goddard has something——"

"An honourable prospect!" exclaimed Mr. Ambrose, growing more and more excited. "To marry a woman ten years older than yourself because she has a little money of her own! You! I would not have thought it of you, John —indeed I would not!"

Indeed no one was more surprised than John Short himself, when he found himself arguing the possibilities of his marriage with his old tutor. But he was an obstinate young fellow enough and was not inclined to give up the fight easily.

"Really," he objected, "I cannot see anything so very terrible in the idea. I shall certainly make my way in the world. You know that it is not for the sake of her money. Many men have married women ten years older than themselves, and not half so beautiful and charming, I am sure."

"I don't believe it," said the vicar, "and if they have, why it has been very different, that is all. Besides, you have not known Mrs. Goddard a week—positively not more than five days—why, it is madness! Do you mean to tell me that at the end of five days you believe you are seriously attached to a lady you never saw in your life before?"

"I saw her once," said John. "That day when I waked Muggins——"

"Once! Nearly three years ago! I have no patience with you John! That a young fellow of your capabilities should give way to such a boyish fancy! It is absolutely amazing! I thought you were growing to like her society very much, but I did not believe it would come to this!"

"It is nothing to be ashamed of," said John stoutly.

"It is something to be afraid of," answered the vicar.

"Oh, do not be alarmed," retorted John. "I will do nothing rash. You have set my mind at rest in assuring me that she will not marry Mr. Juxon. I shall not think of offering myself to Mrs. Goddard until after the Tripos."

"Offering myself"—how deliciously important the expression sounded to John's own ears! It conveyed such a delightful sense of the possibilities of life when at last he should feel that he was in a position to offer himself to any woman, especially to Mrs. Goddard.

"I have a great mind not to ask you to come down, even if you do turn out senior classic," said the vicar, still fuming with excitement. "But if you put off your rash action until then, you will probably have changed your mind."

"I will never change my mind," said John confidently. It was evident, nevertheless, that if the romance of his life were left to the tender mercies of the Reverend Augustin Ambrose, it was likely to come to an abrupt termination. When the two returned to the society of Mrs. Ambrose, the vicar was still very much agitated and John was plunged in a gloomy melancholy.

CHAPTER X.

The vicar's suspicions were more than realised
and he passed an uncomfortable day after his
interview with John, in debating what he ought
to do, whether he ought to do anything at all,
or whether he should merely hasten his old pupil's
departure and leave matters to take care of
themselves.   He was a very conscientious man,
and he felt that he was responsible for John's
conduct towards Mrs. Goddard, seeing that she
had put herself under his protection, and that
John was almost like one of his family.   His
first impulse was to ask counsel of his wife, but
he rejected the plan, reflecting with great justice
that she was very fond of John and had at first
not been sure of liking Mrs. Goddard; she would
be capable of thinking that the latter had " led
Short on," as she would probably say.   The vicar

did not believe this, and was therefore loath that any one else should. He felt that circumstances had made him Mrs. Goddard's protector, and he was moreover personally attached to her; he would not therefore do or say anything whereby she was likely to appear to any one else in an unfavourable light. It was incredible that she should have given John any real encouragement. Mr. Ambrose wondered whether he ought to warn her of his pupil's madness. But when he thought about that, it seemed unnecessary. It was unlikely that John would betray himself during his present visit, since the vicar had solemnly assured him that there was no possibility of a marriage so far as Mr. Juxon was concerned. It was undoubtedly a very uncomfortable situation but there was evidently nothing to be done; Mr. Ambrose felt that to speak to Mrs. Goddard would be to precipitate matters in a way which could not but cause much humiliation to John Short and much annoyance to herself. He accordingly held his peace, but his upper lip set itself stiffly and his eyes had a combative expression which told his wife that there was something the matter.

After breakfast John went out, on pretence of walking in the garden, and Mr. and Mrs. Ambrose were left alone. The latter, as usual after the morning meal, busied herself about the room, searching out those secret corners which she suspected Susan of having forgotten to dust. The vicar stood looking out of the window. The weather was gray and it seemed likely that there would be a thaw which would spoil the skating.

"I think," said Mrs. Ambrose, "that John is far from well."

"What makes you say that?" inquired the vicar, who was thinking of him at that very moment.

"Anybody might see it. He has no appetite —he ate nothing at breakfast this morning. He looks pale. My dear, that boy will certainly break down."

"I don't believe it," answered Mr. Ambrose still looking out of the window. His hands were in his pockets, thrusting the skirts of his clerical coat to right and left; he slowly raised himself upon his toes and let himself down again, repeating the operation as though it helped him to think.

"That is the way you spoil all your coats, Augustin," said his wife looking at him from behind. "I assure you, my dear, that boy is not well. Poor fellow, all alone at college with nobody to look after him——"

"We have all had to go through that. I do not think it hurts him a bit," said the vicar, slowly removing his hands from his pockets in deference to his wife's suggestion.

"Then what is it, I would like to know? There is certainly something the matter. Now I ask you whether he looks like himself?"

"Perhaps he does look a little tired."

"Tired! There is something on his mind, Augustin. I am positively certain there is something on his mind. Why won't you tell me?"

"My dear——" began the vicar, and then stopped short. He was a very truthful man, and as he knew very well what was the matter with John he was embarrassed to find an answer. "My dear," he repeated, "I do not think he is ill."

"Then I am right," retorted Mrs. Ambrose, triumphantly. "It is just as I thought, there is something on his mind. Don't deny it, Augustin; there is something on his mind."

Mr. Ambrose was silent; he glared fiercely at the window panes.

"Why don't you tell me?" insisted his better half. "I am quite sure you know all about it. Augustin, do you know, or do you not?"

Thus directly questioned the vicar turned sharply round, sweeping the window with his coat tails.

"My dear," he said, shortly, "I do know. Can you not imagine that it may be a matter which John does not care to have mentioned?"

Mrs. Ambrose grew red with annoyance. She had set her heart on finding out what had disturbed John, and the vicar had apparently made up his mind that she should not succeed. Such occurrences were very rare between that happy couple.

"I cannot believe he has done anything wrong," said Mrs. Ambrose. "Anything which need be concealed from me—the interest I have always taken——"

"He has not done anything wrong," said the

vicar impatiently. " I do wish you would drop the subject——"

" Then why should it be concealed from me ? " objected his wife with admirable logic. " If it is anything good he need not hide his light under a bushel, I should think."

" There are plenty of things which are neither bad nor good," argued the vicar, who felt that if he could draw Mrs. Ambrose into a Socratic discussion he was safe.

" That is a distinct prevarication, Augustin," said she severely. " I am surprised at you."

" Not at all," retorted the vicar. " What has occurred to John is not owing to any fault of his." In his own mind the good man excused himself by saying that John could not have helped falling in love with Mrs. Goddard. But his wife turned quickly upon him.

" That does not prevent what has occurred to him, as you call it, from being good, or more likely bad, to judge from his looks."

" My dear," said Mr. Ambrose, driven to bay, " I entirely decline to discuss the point."

" I thought you trusted me, Augustin."

"So I do—certainly—and I always consult you about my own affairs."

"I think I have as much right to know about John as you have," retorted his wife, who seemed deeply hurt.

"That is a point then which you ought to settle with John," said the vicar. "I cannot betray his confidence, even to you."

"Oh—then he has been making confidences to you?"

"How in the world should I know about his affairs unless he told me?"

"One may see a great many things without being told about them, you know," answered Mrs. Ambrose, assuming a prim expression as she examined a small spot in the tablecloth. The vicar was walking up and down the room. Her speech, which was made quite at random, startled him. She, too, might easily have observed John's manner when he was with Mrs. Goddard; she might have guessed the secret, and have put her own interpretation on John's sudden melancholy.

"What may one see?" asked the vicar quickly.

"I did not say one could see anything," answered his wife. "But from your manner I infer that there really is something to see. Wait a minute—what can it be?"

"Nothing—my dear, nothing," said the vicar desperately.

"Oh, Augustin, I know you so well," said the implacable Mrs. Ambrose. "I am quite sure now, that it is something I have seen. Deny it, my dear."

The vicar was silent and bit his long upper lip as he marched up and down the room.

"Of course—you cannot deny it," she continued. "It is perfectly clear. The very first day he arrived—when you came down from the Hall, in the evening—Augustin, I have got it! It is Mrs. Goddard—now don't tell me it is not. I am quite sure it is Mrs. Goddard. How stupid of me! Is not it Mrs. Goddard?"

"If you are so positive," said the vicar, resorting to a form of defence generally learned in the nursery, "why do you ask me?"

"I insist upon knowing, Augustin, is it, or is it not, Mrs. Goddard?"

"My dear, I positively refuse to answer any more questions," said the vicar with tardy firmness.

"Oh, it is no matter," retorted Mrs. Ambrose in complete triumph, "if it were not Mrs. Goddard of course you would say so at once."

A form of argument so unanswerable, that the vicar hastily left the room feeling that he had basely betrayed John's confidence, and muttering something about intolerable curiosity. Mrs. Ambrose had vanquished her husband, as she usually did on those rare occasions when anything approaching to a dispute arose between them. Having come to the conclusion that "it" was Mrs. Goddard, the remainder of the secret needed no discovery. It was plain that John must be in love with the tenant of the cottage, and it seemed likely that it would devolve upon Mrs. Ambrose to clear up the matter. She was very fond of John and her first impression was that Mrs. Goddard, whom she now again suspected of having foreign blood, had "led him on"—an impression which the vicar had anticipated when he rashly resolved not to tell his wife John's secret. She knew very well that the vicar must have told John his mind in regard to such an attachment, and she easily concluded that he must have done so on the previous evening when John called him into the study. But she had just won a victory over her husband, and she consequently felt that he was weak, probably too weak to save the situation, and it was borne in upon her that she ought to do something immediately. Unhappily she did not see quite clearly what was to be done. She might go straight to Mrs. Goddard and accuse her of having engaged John's affections; but the more she thought of that, the more diffident she grew in regard to the result of such an interview. Curiosity had led her to a certain point, but caution prevented her from going any further. Mrs. Ambrose was very cautious. The habit of living in a small place, feeling that all her actions were watched by the villagers and duly commented upon by them, had made her even more careful than she was by nature. It would be very unwise to bring about a scene with Mrs. Goddard unless she were very sure of the result. Mrs. Goddard was hardly a friend. In Mrs. Ambrose's opinion an acquaintance of two years and a half standing involving almost daily meetings and the constant exchange of civilities did not constitute friendship. Nevertheless the vicar's wife would have been ashamed to own that after such long continued intercourse she was wholly ignorant of Mrs. Goddard's real character; especially as the latter had requested the vicar to tell Mrs. Ambrose her story when she first appeared at Billingsfield. Moreover, as her excitement at the victory she had gained over her husband began to subside, she found herself reviewing mentally the events of the last few days. She remembered distinctly that John had perpetually pursued Mrs. Goddard, and that although the latter seemed to find him agreeable enough, she had never to Mrs. Ambrose's knowledge given him any of those open encouragements in the way of smiles and signals, which in the good lady's mind were classified under the term " flirting." Mrs. Ambrose's ideas of flirtation may have been antiquated; thirty years of Billingsfield in the society of the Reverend Augustin had not contributed to their extension; but, on the whole, they were just. Mrs. Goddard had not flirted with John. It is worthy of notice that in proportion as the difficulties she would enter upon by demanding an explanation from Mrs. Goddard seemed to grow in magnitude, she gradually arrived at the conclusion that it was John's fault.

Half an hour ago, in the flush of triumph she had indignantly denied that anything could be John's fault. She now resolved to behave to him with great austerity. Such an occurrence as his falling in love could not be passed over with indifference. It seemed best that he should leave Billingsfield very soon.

John thought so too. Existence would not be pleasant now that the vicar knew his secret, and he cursed the folly and curiosity which had led him to betray himself in order to find out whether Mr. Juxon thought of marrying Mrs. Goddard. He had now resolved to return to Cambridge at once and to work his hardest until the Tripos was over. He would then come back to Billingsfield and, with his honours fresh upon him and the prospect of immediate success before him, he would throw himself at Mrs. Goddard's feet. But of course he must have one farewell interview. Oh, those farewell interviews! Those leave-takings, wherein often so much is taken without leave!

Accordingly at luncheon he solemnly announced his intention of leaving the vicarage on the morrow. Mrs. Ambrose received the news with an equanimity which made John suspicious, for she had heretofore constantly pressed him to extend his holiday, expressing the greatest solicitude for his health. She now sat stony as a statue and said very coldly that she was sorry he had to go so soon, but that, of course, it could not be helped. The vicar was moved by his wife's apparent indifference. John, he said, might at least have stayed till the end of the promised week; but at this suggestion Mrs. Ambrose darted at her husband a look so full of fierce meaning, that the vicar relapsed into silence, returning to the consideration of bread and cheese and a salad of mustard and cress. John saw the look and was puzzled; he did not believe the vicar capable of going straight to Mrs.

Ambrose with the story of the last night's interview. But he was already so much disturbed that he did not attempt to explain to himself what was happening.

But when lunch was over, and he realised that he had declared his intention of leaving Billingsfield on the next day, he saw that if he meant to see Mrs. Goddard before he left he must go to her at once. He therefore waited until he heard Mr. and Mrs. Ambrose talking together in the sitting-room and then slipped quietly out by the garden to the road.

He had no idea what he should say when he met Mrs. Goddard. He meant, of course to let her understand, or at least suppose, that he was leaving suddenly on her account, but he did not know in the least how to accomplish it. He trusted that the words necessary to him would come into his head spontaneously. His heart beat fast and he was conscious that he blushed as he rang the bell of the cottage. Almost before he knew where he was, he found himself ushered into the little drawing-room and in the presence of the woman he now felt sure that he loved.

But to his great annoyance she was not alone; Nellie was with her. Mrs. Goddard sat near the fire, reading a review; Nellie was curled up in a corner of the deep sofa with a book, her thick brown curls falling all over her face and hands as she read. Mrs. Goddard extended her hand, without rising.

"How do you do, Mr. Short?" she said. The young man stood hat in hand in the middle of the room, feeling very nervous. It was strange that he should experience any embarrassment now, considering how many hours he had spent in her company during the last few days. He blushed and stammered.

"How do you do? I, in fact—I have come to say good-bye," he blurted out.

"So soon?" said Mrs. Goddard calmly. "Pray sit down."

"Are you really going away, Mr. Short?" asked Nellie. "We are so sorry to lose you." The child had caught the phrase from a book she had been reading, and thought it very appropriate. Her mother smiled.

"Yes—as Nellie says—we are sorry to lose

you," she said. "I thought you were to stay until Monday?"

"So I was—but—very urgent business—not exactly business of course, but work—calls me away sooner." Having delivered himself of this masterpiece of explanation John looked nervously at Nellie and then at his hat and then, with an imploring glance, at Mrs. Goddard.

"But we shall hear of you, Mr. Short—after the examinations, shall we not?"

"Oh yes," said John eagerly. "I will come down as soon as the lists are out."

"You have my best wishes, you know," said Mrs. Goddard kindly. "I feel quite sure that you will really be senior classic."

"Mamma is always saying that—it is quite true," explained Nellie.

John blushed again and looked gratefully at Mrs. Goddard. He wished Nellie would go away, but there was not the least chance of that.

"Yes," said Mrs. Goddard, "I often say it. We all take a great interest in your success here."

"You are very kind," murmured John. "Of

course I shall come down at once and tell you all about it, if I succeed. I do not really expect to be first, of course. I shall be satisfied if I get a place in the first ten. But I mean to do my best."

"No one can do more," said Mrs. Goddard, leaning back in her chair and looking into the fire. Her face was quiet, but not sad as it sometimes was. There was a long silence which John did not know how to break. Nellie sat upon a carved chair by the side of the fireplace dangling her legs and looking at her toes, turning them alternately in and out. She wished John would go for she wanted to get back to her book, but had been told it was not good manners to read when there were visitors. John looked at Mrs. Goddard's face and was about to speak, and then changed his mind and grew red and said nothing. Had she noticed his shyness she would have made an effort at conversation, but she was absent-minded to-day and was thinking of something else. Suddenly she started and laughed a little.

"I beg your pardon," she said. "What were you saying, Mr. Short?" Had John been saying anything he would have repeated it, but being thus interrogated he grew doubly embarrassed.

"I—I have not much to say—except good-bye," he answered.

"Oh, don't go yet," said Mrs. Goddard. "You are not going this afternoon? It is always so unpleasant to say good-bye, is not it?"

"Dreadfully," answered John. "I would rather say anything else in the world. No; I am going early to-morrow morning. There is no help for it," he added desperately. "I must go, you know."

"The next time you come, you will be able to stay much longer," said Mrs. Goddard in an encouraging way. "You will have no more terms, then."

"No indeed—nothing but to take my degree."

"And what will you do then? You said the other day that you thought seriously of going into the church."

"Oh mamma," interrupted Nellie suddenly looking up, "fancy Mr. Short in a black gown, preaching like Mr. Ambrose! How perfectly ridiculous he would look!"

"Nellie—Nellie!" exclaimed Mrs. Goddard, "do not talk nonsense. It is very rude to say Mr. Short would look ridiculous."

"I didn't mean to be rude, mamma," returned Nellie, blushing scarlet and pouting her lips, "only it would be very funny, wouldn't it?"

"I daresay it would," said John, relieved by the interruption. "I wish you would advise me what to do, Mrs. Goddard," he added in a confidential tone.

"I?" she exclaimed, and then laughed. "How should I be able to advise you?"

"I am sure you could," said John, insisting. "You have such wonderfully good judgment——"

"Have I? I did not know it. But, tell me, if you come out very high are you not sure of getting a fellowship?"

"It is likely," answered John indifferently. "But I should have to give it up if I married——"

"Surely, Mr. Short," cried Mrs. Goddard, with a laugh that cut him to the quick, "you do not think of marrying for many years to come?'

"Oh—I don't know," he said, blushing violently, " why should not I ? "

" In the first place, a man should never marry until he is at least five and twenty years old," said Mrs. Goddard, calmly.

" Well—I may be as old as that before I get the fellowship."

" Yes, I daresay.   But even then, why should you want to resign a handsome independence as soon as you have got it ?   Is there anything else so good within your reach ? "

" There is the church, of course," said John. " But Miss Nellie seems to think that ridiculous——"

" Never mind Nellie," answered Mrs. Goddard. " Seriously, Mr. Short, do you approve of entering the church merely as a profession, a means of earning money ? "

" Well—no—I did not put it in that way. But many people do."

" That does not prove that it is either wise or decent," said Mrs. Goddard.   " If you felt impelled to take orders from other motives, it would be different.   As I understand you, you are choosing a profession for the sake of becoming independent."

" Certainly," said John.

" Well, then, there is nothing better for you to do than to get a fellowship and hold it as long as you can, and during that time you can make up your mind." She spoke with conviction, and the plan seemed good. " But I cannot imagine," she continued, " why you should ask my advice."

" And not to marry ?" inquired John nervously.

" There is plenty of time to think of that when you are thirty—even five and thirty is not too late."

" Dear me !" exclaimed John, " I think that is much too old ? "

" Do you call me old ? " asked Mrs. Goddard serenely. " I was thirty-one on my last birth-day."

For the twentieth time, John felt himself growing uncomfortably hot. Not only had he said an unconscionably stupid thing, but Mrs. Goddard, after advising him not to marry for ten years, had almost hinted that she might meanwhile be married herself. What else could she mean by the remark? But John was hardly a responsible being on that day. His views of life and his understanding were equally disturbed.

"No indeed," he protested on hearing her confession of age. "No indeed—why, you are the youngest person I ever saw, of course. But with men—it is quite different."

"Is it? I always thought women were supposed to grow old faster than men. That is the reason why women always marry men so much older than themselves."

"Oh—in that case—I have nothing more to say," replied John in very indistinct tones. The perspiration was standing upon his forehead; the room swam with him and he felt a terrible, prickly sensation all over his body.

"Mamma, shan't I open the door? Mr. Short is so very hot," said Nellie looking at him in some astonishment. At that moment John felt as though he could have eaten little Nellie, long legs, ringlets and all, with infinite satisfaction. He rose suddenly to his feet.

"The fact is—it is late—I must really be saying good-bye," he stammered.

"Must you?" said Mrs. Goddard, suspecting that something was the matter. "Well, I am very sorry to say good-bye. But you will be coming back soon, will you not?"

"Yes—I don't know—perhaps I shall not come back at all. Good-bye—Mrs. Goddard—good-bye, Miss Nellie."

"Good-bye, Mr. Short," said Mrs. Goddard, looking at him with some anxiety. "You are not ill? What is the matter?"

"Oh dear no, nothing," answered John with an unnatural laugh. "No thank you—good-bye."

He managed to get out of the door and rushed down to the road. The cold air steadied his nerves. He felt better. With a sudden revulsion of feeling, he began to utter inward imprecations against his folly, against the house he had just left, against everybody and everything in general, not forgetting poor little Nellie.

"If ever I cross that threshold again—" he muttered with tragic emphasis. His face was still red, and he swung his stick ferociously as he strode towards the vicarage. Several little boys in ragged smock-frocks saw him and thought he had had some beer, even as their own fathers, and made vulgar gestures when his back was turned.

So poor John packed his portmanteau and left the vicarage early on the following morning.   He sent an excuse to Mr. Juxon explaining that the urgency of his work called him back sooner than he had expected, and when the train moved fairly off towards Cambridge he felt that in being spared the ordeal of shaking hands with his rival he had at least escaped some of the bitterness of his fate; as he rolled along he thought very sadly of all that had happened in that short time which was to have been so gay and which had come to such a miserable end.

Reflecting calmly upon his last interview with Mrs. Goddard, he was surprised to find that his memory failed him.   He could not recall anything which could satisfactorily account for the terrible disappointment and distress he had felt.   She had only said that she was thirty-one years old, precisely as the vicar had stated on the previous evening, and she had advised him not to marry for some years to come. But she had laughed, and his feelings had been deeply wounded—he could not tell precisely at what point in the conversation, but he was quite certain that she had laughed, and oh! that terrible Nellie! It was very bitter, and John felt that the best part of his life was lived out. He went back to his books with a dark and melancholy tenacity of purpose, flavoured by a hope that he might come to some sudden and awful end in the course of the next fortnight, thereby causing untold grief and consternation to the hard-hearted woman he had loved. But before the fortnight had expired he found to his surprise that he was intensely interested in his work, and once or twice he caught himself wondering how Mrs. Goddard would look when he went back to Billingsfield and told her he had come out at the head of the classical Tripos—though, of course, he had no intention of going there, nor of ever seeing her again

CHAPTER XI.

Mr. Juxon was relieved to hear that John Short
had suddenly gone back to Cambridge. He had
indeed meant to like him from the first and had
behaved towards him with kindness and hospitality; but while ready to admire his good qualities
and to take a proper amount of interest in his
approaching contest for honours, he had found
him a troublesome person to deal with and, in
his own words, a nuisance. Matters had come
to a climax after the tea at the cottage, when the
squire had so completely vanquished him, but
since that evening the two had not met.

The opposition which John brought to bear
against Mr. Juxon was not, however, without its
effect. The squire was in that state of mind in
which a little additional pressure sufficed to sway
his resolutions. It has been seen that he had

for some time regarded Mrs. Goddard's society as an indispensable element in his daily life; he had been so much astonished at discovering this that he had absented himself for several days and had finally returned ready to submit to his fate, in so far as his fate required that he should see Mrs. Goddard every day. Shortly afterwards John had appeared and by his persistent attempts to monopolise Mrs. Goddard's conversation had again caused an interruption in the squire's habits, which the latter had resented with characteristic firmness. The very fact of having resisted John had strengthened and given a new tone to Mr. Juxon's feelings towards his tenant. He began to watch the hands of the clock with more impatience than formerly when, after breakfast, he sat reading the papers before the library fire, waiting for the hour when he was accustomed to go down to the cottage. His interest in the papers decreased as his interest in the time of day grew stronger, and for the first time in his life he found to his great surprise that after reading the news of the day with the greatest care, he was often quite unable to remember a word of what he had read. Then, at first, he would be angry with himself and would impose upon himself the task of reading the paper again before going to the cottage. But very soon he found that he had to read it twice almost every day, and this seemed such an unreasonable waste of time that he gave it up, and fell into very unsystematic habits.

For some days, as though by mutual consent, neither Mrs. Goddard nor the squire spoke of John Short. The squire was glad he was gone and hoped that he would not come back, but was too kind-hearted to say so; Mrs. Goddard instinctively understood Mr. Juxon's state of mind and did not disturb his equanimity by broaching an unpleasant subject. Several days passed by after John had gone and he would certainly not have been flattered had he known that during that time two, out of the four persons he had met so often in his short holiday, had never so much as mentioned him.

One afternoon in January the squire found himself alone with Mrs. Goddard. It was a great exception, and she herself doubted whether

she were wise to receive him when she had not
Nellie with her.   Nellie had gone to the vicarage
to help Mrs. Ambrose with some work she had
in hand for her poor people, but Mrs. Goddard
had a slight headache and had stayed at home in
consequence.   The weather was very bad; heavy
clouds were driving overhead and the north-east
wind howled and screamed through the leafless
oaks of the park, driving a fine sleet against the
cottage windows and making the dead creepers
rattle against the wall.   It was a bitter January
day, and Mrs. Goddard felt how pleasant a thing
it was to stay at home with a book beside her
blazing fire.   She was all alone, and Nellie would
not be back before four o'clock.   Suddenly a
well-known step echoed upon the slate flags
without and there was a ring at the bell.   Mrs.
Goddard had hardly time to think what she
should do, as she laid her book upon her knee
and looked nervously over her shoulder towards
the door.   It was awkward, she thought, but it
could not be helped.   In such weather it seemed
absurd to send the squire away because her little
girl was not with her.   He had come all the way

down from the Hall to spend this dreary afternoon at the cottage—she could not send him away. There were sounds in the passage as of some one depositing a waterproof coat and an umbrella, the door opened and Mr. Juxon appeared upon the threshold.

"Come in," said Mrs. Goddard, banishing her scruples as soon as she saw him. "I am all alone," she added rather apologetically. The squire, who was a simple man in many ways, understood the remark and felt slightly embarrassed.

"Is Miss Nellie out?" he asked, coming forward and taking Mrs. Goddard's hand. He had not yet reached the point of calling the child plain "Nellie;" he would have thought it an undue familiarity.

"She is gone to the vicarage," answered Mrs. Goddard. "What a dreadful day! You must be nearly frozen. Will you have a cup of tea?"

"No thanks—no, you are very kind. I have had a good walk; I am not cold—never am. As you say, in such weather I could not resist the temptation to come in. This is a capital day to test that India-rubber tubing we have put round your windows. Excuse me—I will just look and see if the air comes through."

Mr. Juxon carefully examined the windows of the sitting-room and then returned to his seat.

"It is quite air-tight, I think," he said with some satisfaction, as he smoothed his hair with his hand.

"Oh, quite," said Mrs. Goddard. "It was so very good of you."

"Not a bit of it," returned the squire cheerily. "A landlord's chief pre-occupation ought to be the comfort of his tenants and his next thought should be to keep his houses in repair. I never owned any houses before, so I have determined to start with good principles."

"I am sure you succeed. You walked down?"

"Always walk, in any weather. It is much less trouble and much cheaper. Besides, I like it."

"The best of all reasons. Then you will not have any tea? I almost wish you would, because I want some myself."

"Oh of course—in that case I shall be delighted. Shall I ring?"

He rang and Martha brought the tea. Some time was consumed in the preparations which Mr. Juxon watched with interest as though he had never seen tea made before. Everything that Mrs. Goddard did interested him.

"I do not know why it is," she said at last, " but weather like this is delightful when one is safe at home. I suppose it is the contrast——"

" Yes indeed. It is like the watch below in dirty weather."

" Excuse me—I don't quite understand——"

" At sea," explained the squire. " There is no luxury like being below when the decks are wet and there is heavy weather about."

"I should think so," said Mrs. Goddard. " Have you been at sea much, Mr. Juxon ? "

" Thirty years," returned the squire laconically. Mrs. Goddard looked at him in astonishment.

" You don't mean to say you have been a sailor all your life ? "

" Does that surprise you ? I have been a sailor since I was twelve years old. But I got very tired of it. It is a hard life."

" Were you in the navy, Mr. Juxon ? " asked

Mrs. Goddard eagerly, feeling that she was at last upon the track of some information in regard to his past life.

"Yes—I was in the navy," answered the squire, slowly. "And then I was at college, and then in the navy again. At last I entered the merchant service and commanded my own ships for nearly twenty years."

"How very extraordinary! Why then, you must have been everywhere."

"Very nearly. But I would much rather be in Billingsfield."

"You never told me," said Mrs. Goddard almost reproachfully. "What a change it must have been for you, from the sea to the life of a country gentleman!"

"It is what I always wanted."

"But you do not seem at all like the sea captains one hears about——"

"Well, perhaps not," replied the squire thoughtfully. "There are a great many different classes of sea captains. I always had a taste for books. A man can read a great deal on a long voyage. I have sometimes been at sea for more than two years at a time. Besides, I had a fairly good education and—well, I suppose it was because I was a gentleman to begin with and was more than ten years in the Royal Navy. All that makes a great difference. Have you ever made a long voyage, Mrs. Goddard?"

"I have crossed the chánnel," said she. "But I wish you would tell me something more about your life."

"Oh no—it is very dull, all that. You always make me talk about myself," said the squire in a tone of protestation.

"It is very interesting."

"But—could not we vary the conversation by talking about you a little," suggested Mr. Juxon.

"Oh no! Please—" exclaimed Mrs. Goddard rather nervously. She grew pale and busied herself again with the tea. "Do tell me more about your voyages. I suppose that was the way you collected so many beautiful things, was it not?"

"Yes, I suppose so," answered the squire, looking at her curiously. "In fact of course it was. I was a great deal in China and South

America and India, and in all sorts of places where one picks up things."

"And in Turkey, too, where you got Stamboul?"

"Yes. He was so wet that I left him outside to-day. Did not want to spoil your carpet."

The squire had a way of turning the subject when he seemed upon the point of talking about himself which was very annoying to Mrs. Goddard. But she had not entirely recovered her equanimity and for the moment had lost control of the squire. Besides she had a headache that day.

"Stamboul does not get the benefit of the contrast we were talking about at first," she remarked, in order to say something.

"I could not possibly bring him in," returned the squire looking at her again. "Excuse me, Mrs. Goddard—I don't mean to be inquisitive you know, but—I always want to be of any use."

She looked at him inquiringly.

"I mean, to be frank, I am afraid that something is giving you trouble. I have noticed it for some time. You know, if I can be of any use, if I can help you in any way—you have only to say the word."

Again she looked at him. She did not know why it was so, but the genuinely friendly tone in which he made the offer touched her. She was surprised, however; she could not understand why he should think she was in trouble, and indeed she was in no greater distress than she had suffered during the greater part of the last three years.

"You are very kind, Mr. Juxon. But there is nothing the matter—I have a headache."

"Oh," said the squire, "I beg your pardon." He looked away and seemed embarrassed.

"You have done too much already," said Mrs. Goddard, fearing that she had not sufficiently acknowledged his offer of assistance.

"I cannot do too much. That is impossible," he said in a tone of conviction. "I have very few friends, Mrs. Goddard, and I like to think that you are one of the best of them."

"I am sure—I dont know what to say, Mr. Juxon," she answered, somewhat startled by the directness of his speech. I am sure you have always been most kind, and I hope you do not think me ungrateful."

"I? You? No—dear me, please never mention it! The fact is, Mrs. Goddard—" he stopped and smoothed her hair. "What particularly disagreeable weather," he remarked irrelevantly, looking out of the window at the driving sleet.

Mrs. Goddard looked down and slowly stirred her tea. She was pale and her hand trembled a little, but no one could have guessed that she was suffering any strong emotion. Mr. Juxon looked towards the window, and the gray light of the winter's afternoon fell coldly upon his square sunburned face and carefully trimmed beard. He was silent for a moment, and then, still looking away from his companion, he continued in a less hesitating tone.

"The fact is, I have been thinking a great deal of late," he said, "and it has struck me that your friendship has grown to be the most important thing in my life." He paused again and turned his hat round upon his knee. Still Mrs. Goddard said nothing, and as he did not look at her he did not perceive that she was unnaturally agitated.

"I have told you what my life has been," he continued presently. I have been a sailor. I made a little money. I finally inherited my uncle's estate here. I will tell you anything else you would like to ask—I don't think I ever did anything to conceal. I am forty-two years old. I have about five thousand a year and I am naturally economical. I would like to make you a proposal—a very respectful proposal, Mrs. Goddard——"

Mrs. Goddard uttered a faint exclamation of surprise and fell back in her chair, staring with wide eyes at the squire, her cheeks very pale and her lips white. He was too much absorbed in what he was saying to notice the short smothered ejaculation, and he was too much embarrassed to look at her.

"Mrs. Goddard," he said, his voice trembling slightly, "will you marry me?"

He was not prepared for the result of his speech. He had pondered it for some time and had come to the conclusion that it was best to say as little as possible and to say it plainly. It was an honourable proposal of marriage from a man in middle life to a lady he had known and respected for many months; there was very little romance about it; he did not intend that there should be any. As soon as he had spoken he turned his head and looked to her for his answer. Mrs. Goddard had clasped her small white hands over her face and had turned her head away from him against the cushion of the high backed chair. The squire felt very uncomfortable in the dead silence, broken only by the sleet driving against the window panes with a hissing, rattling sound, and by the singing of the tea-kettle. For some seconds, which to Juxon seemed like an eternity, Mrs. Goddard did not move. At last she suddenly dropped her hands and looked into the squire's eyes. He was startled by the ashen hue of her face.

"It is impossible," she said, shortly, in broken tones. But the squire was prepared for some difficulties.

"I do not see the impossibility," he said quite calmly. "Of course, I would not press you for an answer, my dear Mrs. Goddard. I am afraid I have been very abrupt, but I will go away, I will leave you to consider——"

"Oh no, no!" cried the poor lady in great distress. "It is quite impossible—I assure you it is quite, quite impossible!"

"I don't know," said Mr. Juxon, who saw that she was deeply moved, but was loath to abandon the field without a further struggle. "I am not a very young man, it is true—but I am not a very old one either. You, my dear Mrs. Goddard, have been a widow for some years ——"

"I?" cried Mrs. Goddard with a wild hysterical laugh. "I! Oh God of mercy! I wish I were." Again she buried her face in the cushion. Her bosom heaved violently.

The squire started as though he had been struck, and the blood rushed to his brown face so that the great veins on his temples stood out like cords.

"Did I—did I understand you to say that —your husband is living?" he asked in a strong, loud voice, ringing with emotion.

Mrs. Goddard moved a little and seemed to make a great effort to speak.

"Yes," she said very faintly. The squire rose to his feet and paced the room in terrible agitation.

"But where?" he asked, stopping suddenly in his walk. "Mrs. Goddard, I think I have a right to ask where he is—why you have never spoken of him?"

By a supreme effort the unfortunate lady raised herself from her seat supporting herself upon one hand, and faced the squire with wildly staring eyes.

"You have a right to know," she said. "He is in Portland—sentenced to twelve years hard labour for forgery."

She said it all, to the end, and then fell back into her chair. But she did not hide her face this time. The fair pathetic features were quite motionless and white, without any expression, and her hands lay with the palms turned upwards on her knees.

Charles James Juxon was a man of few words, not given to using strong language on any occasion. But he was completely overcome by the horror of the thing. He turned icy cold as he stood still, rooted to the spot, and he uttered aloud one strong and solemn ejaculation, more an invocation than an oath, as though he called on heaven to witness the misery he looked upon. He gazed at the colourless, inanimate face of the poor lady and walked slowly to the window. There he stood for fully five minutes, motionless, staring out at the driving sleet.

Mrs. Goddard had fainted away, but it did not occur to the squire to attempt to recall her to her senses. It seemed merciful that she should have lost consciousness even for a moment. Indeed she needed no help, for in a few minutes she slowly opened her eyes and closed them, then opened them again and saw Mr. Juxon's figure darkening the window against the gray light.

"Mr. Juxon," she said faintly, "come here, please."

The squire started and turned. Then he came and sat down beside her. His face was very stern and grave, and he said nothing.

"Mr. Juxon," said Mrs. Goddard, speaking in

a low voice, but with far more calm than he could have expected, "you have a right to know my story. You have been very kind to me, you have made an honourable offer to me, you have said you were my friend. I ought to have told you before. If I had had any idea of what was passing in your mind, I would have told you, cost what it might."

Mr. Juxon gravely bowed his head. She was quite right, he thought. He had a right to know all. With all his kind-heartedness he was a stern man by nature.

"Yes," continued Mrs. Goddard, "you have every right to know. My husband," her voice trembled, "was the head of an important firm in London. I was the only child of his partner. Not long after my father's death I married Mr. Goddard. He was an extravagant man of brilliant tastes. I had a small fortune of my own which my father had settled upon me, independent of his share in the firm. My guardians, of whom my husband was one, advised me to leave my father's fortune in the concern. When I came of age, a year after my marriage, I agreed to do it. My husband—I never knew it till long afterwards—was very rash. He speculated on the Exchange and tampered with the deposits placed in his hands. We lived in great luxury. I knew nothing of his affairs. Three years ago, after we had been married nearly ten years, the firm failed. It was a fraudulent bankruptcy. My husband fled but was captured and brought back. It appeared that at the last moment, in the hope of retrieving his position and saving the firm, he had forged the name of one of his own clients for a large amount. We had a country place at Putney which he had given to me. I sold it, with all my jewels and most of my possessions. I would have given up everything I possessed, but I thought of Nellie—poor little Nellie. The lawyers assured me that I ought to keep my own little fortune. I kept about five hundred a year. It is more than I need, but it seemed very little then. The lawyer who conducted the defence, such as it was, advised me to go abroad, but I would not. Then he spoke of Mr. Ambrose, who had educated his son, and gave me a note to him. I came here and I told

Mr. Ambrose my whole story. I only wanted to be alone—I thought I did right——"

Her courage had sustained her so far, but it had been a great effort. Her voice trembled and broke and at last the tears began to glisten in her eyes.

"Does Nellie know?" asked the squire, who had sat very gravely by her side, but who was in reality deeply moved.

"No — she thinks he — that he is dead," faltered Mrs. Goddard. Then she fairly burst into tears and sobbed passionately, covering her face and rocking herself from side to side.

"My dear friend," said Mr. Juxon very kindly and laying one hand upon her arm, "pray try and calm yourself. Forgive me—I beg you to forgive me for having caused you so much pain——"

"Do you still call me a friend?" sobbed the poor lady.

"Indeed I do," quoth the squire stoutly. And he meant it. Mrs. Goddard dropped her hands and stared into the fire through her falling tears.

"I think you behaved very honourably—very

generously," continued Mr. Juxon, who did not know precisely how to console her, and indeed stood much in need of consolation himself. "Perhaps I had better leave you—you are very much agitated—you must need rest—would you not rather that I should go?"

"Yes—it is better," said she, still staring at the fire. "You know all about me now," she added in a tone of pathetic regret. The squire rose to his feet.

"I hope," he said with some hesitation, "that this—this very unfortunate day will not prevent our being friends—better friends than before?"

Mrs. Goddard looked up gratefully through her tears.

"How good you are!" she said softly.

"Not at all—I am not at all good—I only want to be your friend. Good-bye—G—God bless you!" He seized her hand and squeezed it and then hurried out of the room. A moment later he was crossing the road with Stamboul, who was very tired of waiting, bounding before him.

The squire was not a romantic character.

He was a strong plain man, who had seen the world and was used to most forms of danger and to a good many forms of suffering. He was kind-hearted and generous, capable of feeling sincere sympathy for others, and under certain circumstances of being deeply wounded himself. He had indeed a far more refined nature than he himself suspected and on this memorable day he had experienced more emotions than he remembered to have felt in the course of many years.

After long debate and after much searching inquiry into his own motives he had determined to offer himself to Mrs. Goddard, and he had accordingly done so in his own straightforward manner. It had seemed a very important action in his life, a very solemn step, but he was not prepared for the acute sense of disappointment which he felt when Mrs. Goddard first said it was impossible for her to accept him, still less had he anticipated the extraordinary story which she had told him, in explanation of her refusal. His ideas were completely upset. That Mrs. Goddard was not a widow after all, was almost as astounding as that she should prove to be the wife of a felon. But Mr. Juxon was no less persuaded that she herself was a perfectly good and noble woman, than he had been before. He felt that he would like to cut the throat of the villain himself; but he resolved that he would more than ever try to be a good friend to Mrs. Goddard.

He walked slowly through the storm towards his house, his broad figure facing the wind and sleet with as much ease as a steamer forging against a head sea. He was perfectly indifferent to the weather; but Stamboul slunk along at his heels, shielding himself from the driving wet snow behind his master's sturdy legs. The squire was very much disturbed. The sight of his own solemn butler affected him strangely. He stared about the library in a vacant way, as though he had never seen the place before. The realisation of his own calm and luxurious life seemed unnatural, and his thoughts went back to the poor weeping woman he had just left. She, too, had enjoyed all this, and more also. She had probably been richer than he.

And now she was living on five hundred a year in one of his own cottages, hiding her shame in desolate Billingsfield, the shame of her husband, the forger.

It was such a hopeless position, the squire thought. No one could help her, no one could do anything for her. For many weeks, revolving the situation in his mind, he had amused himself by thinking how she would look when she should be mistress of the Hall, and wondering whether little Nellie would call him " father," or merely " Mr. Juxon." And now, she turned out to be the wife of a forger, sentenced to hard labour in a convict prison, for twelve years. For twelve years—nearly three must have elapsed already. In nine years more Goddard would be out again. Would he claim his wife? Of course—he would come back to her for support. And poor little Nellie thought he was dead! It would be a terrible day when she had to be told. If he only would die in prison!—but men sentenced to hard labour rarely die. They are well cared for. It is a healthy life. He would certainly live through it and come back to claim his wife.

Poor Mrs. Goddard! her troubles were not ended yet, though the State had provided her with a respite of twelve years.

The squire sat long in his easy-chair in the great library, and forgot to dress for dinner—he always dressed, even though he was quite alone. But the solemn face of his butler betrayed neither emotion nor surprise when the master of the Hall walked into the dining-room in his knickerbockers.

CHAPTER XII.

WHEN Nellie came home from the vicarage she found her mother looking very ill. There were dark rings under her eyes, and her features were drawn and tear-stained, while the beautiful waves of her brown hair had lost their habitual neatness and symmetry. The child noticed these things, with a child's quickness, but explained them on the ground that her mother's headache was probably much worse. Mrs. Goddard accepted the explanation and on the following day Nellie had forgotten all about it; but her mother remembered it long, and it was many days before she recovered entirely from the shock of her interview with the squire. The latter did not come to see her as usual, but on the morning after his visit he sent her down a package of books and some orchids from his hothouses.

He thought it best to leave her to herself for a little while ; the very sight of him, he argued, would be painful to her, and any meeting with her would be painful to himself. He did not go out of the house, but spent the whole day in his library among his books, not indeed reading, but pretending to himself that he was very busy. Being a strong and sensible man he did not waste time in bemoaning his sorrows, but he thought about them long and earnestly. The more he thought, the more it appeared to him that Mrs. Goddard was the person who deserved pity rather than he himself. His mind dwelt on the terrors of her position in case her husband should return and claim his wife and daughter when the twelve years were over, and he thought with·horror of Nellie's humiliation, if at the age of twenty she should discover that her father during all these years had not been honourably dead and buried, but had been suffering the punishment of a felon in Portland. That the only attempt he had ever made to enter the matrimonial state should have been so singularly unfortunate was indeed a matter which caused him sincere sorrow; he had thought too often of being married to Mary Goddard to be able to give up the idea without a sigh. But it is due to him to say that in the midst of his own disappointment he thought much more of her sorrows than of his own, a state of mind most probably due to his temperament.

He saw also how impossible it was to console Mrs. Goddard or even to alleviate the distress of mind which she must constantly feel. Her destiny was accomplished in part, and the remainder seemed absolutely inevitable. No one could prevent her husband from leaving his prison when his crime was expiated; and no one could then prevent him from joining his wife and ending his life under her roof. At least so it seemed. Endless complications would follow. Mrs. Goddard would certainly have to leave Billingsfield—no one could expect the Ambroses or the squire himself to associate with a convict forger. Mr. Juxon vaguely wondered whether he should live another nine years to see the end of all this, and he inwardly determined to go to sea again rather than to witness such misery.

He could not see, no one could see how things could possibly turn out in any other way. It would have been some comfort to have gone to the vicar, and to have discussed with him the possibilities of Mrs. Goddard's future. The vicar was a man after his own heart, honest, reliable, charitable and brave; but Mr. Juxon thought that it would not be quite loyal towards Mrs. Goddard if he let any one else know that he was acquainted with her story.

For two days he stayed at home and then he went to see her. To his surprise she received him very quietly, much as she usually did, without betraying any emotion; whereupon he wished that he had not allowed two days to pass without making his usual visit. Mrs. Goddard almost wished so too. She had been so much accustomed to regard the squire as a friend, and she had so long been used to the thought that Mr. and Mrs. Ambrose knew of her past trouble, that the fact of the squire becoming acquainted with her history seemed to her less important, now that it was accomplished, than it seemed to the squire himself. She had long thought of telling him all; she had seriously contemplated doing so when he first came to Billingsfield, and now at last the thing was done. She was glad of it. She was no longer in a false position; he could never again think of marrying her; they could henceforth meet as friends, since he was so magnanimous as to allow their friendship to exist. Her pride had suffered so terribly in the beginning that it was past suffering now. She felt that she was in the position of a suppliant asking only for a quiet resting-place for herself and her daughter, and she was grateful to the people who gave her what she asked, feeling that she had fallen among good Samaritans, whereas in merry England it would have been easy for her to have fallen among priests and Pharisees.

So it came about that in a few days her relations with Mr. Juxon were re-established upon a new basis, but more firmly and satisfactorily than before, seeing that now there was no possibility of mistake. And for a long time it seemed as though matters would go on as before. Neither Mrs. Goddard nor the squire ever referred to the interview on that memorable stormy afternoon, and so far as the squire could judge his life and hers might go on with perfect tranquillity until it should please the powers that be and the governor of Portland to set Mr. Walter Goddard at liberty. Heaven only knew what would happen then, but it was provided that there should be plenty of time to prepare for anything which might ensue. The point upon which Mrs. Goddard had not spoken plainly was that which concerned her probable treatment of her husband after his liberation. She had passed that question over in silence. She had probably never dared to decide. Most probably she would at the last minute seek some safer retreat than Billingsfield and make up her mind to hide for the rest of her life. But Mr. Juxon had heard of women who had carried charity as far as to receive back their husbands under even worse circumstances; women were soft-hearted creatures, reflected the squire, and capable of anything.

Few people in such a situation could have acted consistently as though nothing had happened. But Mr. Juxon's extremely reticent nature found it easy to bury other people's important secrets at least as deeply as he buried the harmless details of his own honest life. Not a hair of his smooth head was ruffled, not a line of his square manly face was disturbed. He looked and acted precisely as he had looked and acted before. His butler remarked that he ate a little less heartily of late, and that on one evening, as has been recorded, the squire forgot to dress for dinner. But the butler in his day had seen greater eccentricities than these; he had the greatest admiration for Mr. Juxon and was not inclined to cavil at small things. A real gentleman, of the good sort, who dressed for dinner when he was alone, who never took too much wine, who never bullied the servants nor quarrelled unjustly with the bills, was, as the butler expressed it, "not to be sneezed at, on no account." The place was a little dull, but the functionary was well stricken in years and did not like hard work. Mr. Juxon seemed to be conscious that as he never had visitors at the Hall and as there were consequently no "tips," his staff was entitled to an occasional fee, which he presented always with great regularity, and which had the desired effect.   He was a generous man as well as a just.

The traffic in roses and orchids and new books continued as usual between the Hall and the cottage, and for many weeks nothing extraordinary occurred.   Mrs. Ambrose and Mrs. Goddard met frequently, and the only difference to be observed in the manner of the former was that she mentioned John Short very often, and every time she mentioned him she fixed her gray eyes sternly upon Mrs. Goddard, who however did not notice the scrutiny, or, if she did, was not in the least disturbed by it.   For a long time Mrs. Ambrose entertained a feeble intention of addressing Mrs. Goddard directly upon the subject of John's affections, but the longer she put off doing so, the harder it seemed to do it.   Mrs. Ambrose had great faith in the sternness of her eye under certain circumstances, and seeing that Mrs. Goddard never winced, she gradually fell into the belief that John had been the more to blame, if there was any blame in the matter. She had indeed succeeded in the first instance, by methods of her own which have been heretofore detailed, in extracting a sort of reluctant admission from her husband; but since that day he had proved obdurate to all entreaty. Once only he had said with considerable impatience that John was a very silly boy, and was much better engaged with his books at college than in running after Mrs. Goddard. That was all, and gradually as the regular and methodical life at the vicarage effaced the memory of the doings at Christmas time, the good Mrs. Ambrose forgot that anything unpleasant had ever occurred. There was no disturbance of the existing relations and everything went on as before for many weeks. The February thaw set in early and the March winds began to blow before February was fairly out. Nat Barker the octogenarian cripple, who had the reputation of being a weather prophet, was understood to have said that the spring was "loike to be forrard t'year," and the minds of the younger inhabitants were considerably relieved. Not that Nat Barker's prophecies were usually fulfilled; no one ever remembered them at the time when they might have been verified. But they were always made at the season when people had nothing to do but to talk about them. Mr. Thomas Reid, the conservative sexton, turned up his nose at them, and said he "wished Nat Barker had to dig a parish depth grave in three hours without a drop of nothin' to wet his pipe with, and if he didden fine that groun' oncommon owdacious Thomas Reid he didden know. They didden know nothin', sir, them parish cripples." Wherewith the worthy sexton took his way with a battered tin can to get his "fours" at the Feathers. He did not patronise the Duke's Head. It was too new-fangled for him, and he suspected his arch enemy, Mr. Abraham Boosey, of putting a rat or two into the old beer to make it "draw," which accounted for its being so "hard." But Mr. Abraham Boosey was the undertaker, and he, Thomas Reid, was the sexton, and it did not do to express these views too loudly, lest perchance Mr. Boosey should, just in his play, construct a coffin or two just too big for the regulation grave, and thereby leave

Mr. Reid in the lurch. For the undertaker and the gravedigger are as necessary to each other, as Mr. Reid maintained, as a pair of blackbirds in a hedge.

But the spring was "forrard t'year" and the weather was consequently even more detestable than usual at that season. The roads were heavy. The rain seemed never weary of pouring down and the wind never tired of blowing. The wet and leafless creepers beat against the walls of the cottage, and the chimneys smoked both there and at the vicarage. The rooms were pervaded with a disagreeable smell of damp coal smoke, and the fires struggled desperately to burn against the overwhelming odds of rain and wind which came down the chimneys. Mrs. Goddard never remembered to have been so uncomfortable during the two previous winters she had spent in Billingsfield, and even Nellie grew impatient and petulant. The only bright spot in those long days seemed to be made by the regular visits of Mr. Juxon, by the equally regular bi-weekly appearance of the Ambroses when they came to tea, and by the little dinners at the vicarage. The weather had grown so wet and the roads so bad that on these latter occasions the vicar sent his dogcart with Reynolds and the old mare, Strawberry, to fetch his two guests. Even Mr. Juxon, who always walked when he could, had got into the habit of driving down to the cottage in a strange-looking gig which he had imported from America, and which, among all the many possessions of the squire, alone attracted the unfavourable comment of his butler. He would have preferred to see a good English dogcart, high in the seat and wheels, at the door of the Hall, instead of that outlandish vehicle; but Joseph Ruggles, the groom, explained to him that it was easier to clean than a dogcart, and that when it rained he sat inside with the squire.

On a certain evening in February, towards the end of the month, Mr. and Mrs. Ambrose and Mr. Juxon came to have tea with Mrs. Goddard. Mr. Juxon had at first not been regularly invited to these entertainments. They were perhaps not thought worthy of his grandeur; at all events both the vicar's wife and Mrs. Goddard had asked him very rarely. But as time went on and Mr.

Juxon's character developed under the eyes of the little Billingsfield society, it had become apparent to every one that he was a very simple man, making no pretensions whatever to any superiority on account of his station. They grew more and more fond of him, and ended by asking him to their small sociable evenings. On these occasions it generally occurred that the squire and the vicar fell into conversation about classical and literary subjects while the two ladies talked of the little incidents of Billingsfield life, of Tom Judd's wife and baby, of Joe Staines, the choir boy, who was losing his voice, and of similar topics of interest in the very small world in which they lived.

The present evening had not been at all a remarkable one so far as the talk was concerned. The drenching rain, the tendency of the fire to smoke, the general wetness and condensed depravity of the atmosphere had affected the spirits of the little party. They were not gay, and they broke up early. It was not nine o'clock when all had gone, and Mrs. Goddard and little Eleanor were left alone by the side of their drawing-room fire.   The child sat upon a footstool and leaned her head against her mother's knee.   Mrs. Goddard herself was thoughtful and sad, without precisely knowing why.   She generally looked forward with pleasure to meeting the Ambroses, but this evening she had been rather disappointed.   The conversation had dragged, and the excellent Mrs. Ambrose had been more than usually prosy. Nellie had complained of a headache and leaned wearily against her mother's knee.

"Tell me a story, mamma—won't you ?   Like the ones you used to tell me when I was quite a little girl."

"Dear child," said her mother, who was not thinking of story-telling, "I am afraid I have forgotten all the ones I ever knew.   Besides, darling, it is time for you to go to bed."

"I don't want to go to bed, mamma.   It is such a horrid night.   The wind keeps me awake."

"You will not sleep at all if I tell you a story," objected Mrs. Goddard.

"Mr. Juxon tells me such nice stories," said Nellie, reproachfully.

"What are they about, dear ?"

"Oh, his stories are beautiful. They are always about ships and the blue sea and wonderful desert islands where he has been. What a wonderful man he is, mamma, is not he?"

"Yes, dear, he talks very interestingly." Mrs. Goddard stroked Nellie's brown curls and looked into the fire.

"He told me that once, ever so many years ago—he must be very old, mamma—" Nellie paused and looked up inquiringly.

"Well, darling—not so very, very old. I think he is over forty."

"Over forty—four times eleven—he is not four times as old as I am. Almost, though. All his stories are ever so many years ago. He said he was sailing away ever so far, in a perfectly new ship, and the name of the ship was—let me see, what was the name? I think it was——"

Mrs. Goddard started suddenly and laid her hand on the child's shoulder.

"Did you hear anything, Nellie?" she asked quickly. Nellie looked up in some surprise.

"No, mamma. When? Just now? It must have been the wind. It is such a horrid night.

The name of the ship was the 'Zephyr'—I remember, now." She looked up again to see if her mother was listening to the story. Mrs. Goddard looked pale and glanced uneasily towards the closed window. She had probably been mistaken.

"And where did the ship sail to, Nellie dear?" she asked, smoothing the child's curls again and forcing herself to smile.

"Oh—the ship was a perfectly new ship and it was the most beautiful weather in the world. They were sailing away ever so far, towards the straits of Magellan. I was so glad because I knew where the straits of Magellan were—and Mr. Juxon was immensely astonished. But I had been learning about the Terra del Fuego and the people who were frozen there, in my geography that very morning—was not it lucky? So I knew all about it—mamma, how nervous you are! It is nothing but the wind. I wish you would listen to my story——"

"I am listening, darling," said Mrs. Goddard, making a strong effort to overcome her agitation and drawing the child closer to her. "Go on, sweetheart—you were in the straits of Magellan, you said, sailing away——"

" Mr. Juxon was, mamma," said Nellie correcting her mother with the asperity of a child who does not receive all the attention it expects.

" Of course, dear, Mr. Juxon, and the ship was the ' Zephyr.' "

" Yes—the ' Zephyr,' " repeated Nellie, who was easily pacified. " It was at Christmas time he said—but that is summer in the southern hemisphere," she added, proud of her knowledge. " So it was very fine weather. And Mr. Juxon was walking up and down the deck in the afternoon, smoking a cigar——"

" He never smokes, dear," interrupted Mrs. Goddard, glad to show Nellie that she was listening.

" Well, but he did then, because he said so," returned Nellie unmoved. " And as he walked and looked out—sailors always look out, you know—he saw the most wonderful thing, close to the ship—the most wonderful thing he ever saw," added Nellie with some redundance of expression.

"Was it a whale, child?" asked her mother, staring into the fire and trying to pay attention.

"A whale, mamma!" repeated Nellie contemptuously. "As if there were anything remarkable about a whale! Mr. Juxon has seen billions of whales, I am sure."

"Well, what was it, dear?"

"It was the most awfully tremendous thing with green and blue scales, a thousand times as big as the ship—oh mamma! What was that?"

Nellie started up from her stool and knelt beside her mother, looking towards the window. Mrs. Goddard was deathly pale and grasped the arm of her chair.

"Somebody knocked at the window, mamma," said Nellie breathlessly. "And then somebody said 'Mary'—quite loud. Oh mamma, what can it be?"

"Mary?" repeated Mrs. Goddard as though she were in a dream.

"Yes—quite loud. Oh mamma! it must be Mary's young man—he does sometimes come in the evening."

"Mary's young man, child?" Mrs. Goddard's

heart leaped. Her cook's name was Mary, as well as her own. Nellie naturally never associated the name with her mother, as she never heard anybody call her by it.

"Yes mamma. Don't you know? The postman—the man with the piebald horse." The explanation was necessary, as Mrs. Goddard rarely received any letters and probably did not know the postman by sight.

"At this time of night!" exclaimed Mrs. Goddard. "It is too bad. Mary is gone to bed."

"Perhaps he thinks you are gone to the vicarage and that Mary is sitting up for you in the drawing-room," suggested Nellie with much good sense. "Well, he can't come in, can he, mamma?"

"Certainly not," said her mother. "But I think you had much better go to bed, my dear. It is half-past nine." She spoke indistinctly, almost thickly, and seemed to be making a violent effort to control herself. But Nellie had settled down upon her stool again, and did not notice her mother.

"Oh not yet," said she. "I have not nearly finished about the sea-serpent. Mr. Juxon said it was not like anything in the world. Do listen, mamma! It is the most wonderful story you ever heard. It was all covered with blue and green scales, and it rolled, and rolled, and rolled, and rolled, till at last it rolled up against the side of the ship with such a tremendous bump that Mr. Juxon fell right down on his back."

"Yes dear," said Mrs. Goddard mechanically, as the child paused.

"You don't seem to mind at all!" cried Nellie, who felt that her efforts to amuse her mother were not properly appreciated. "He fell right down on his back and hurt himself awfully."

"That was very sad," said Mrs. Goddard. "Did he catch the sea-serpent afterwards?"

"Catch the sea-serpent! Why mamma, don't you know that nobody has ever caught the sea-serpent? Why, hardly anybody has ever seen him, even!"

"Yes dear, but I thought Mr. Juxon——"

. "Of course, Mr. Juxon is the most wonderful man—but he could not catch the sea-serpent. Just fancy! When he got up from his fall, he looked and he saw him quite half a mile away.

He must have gone awfully fast, should not you think so ? Because, you know, it was only a minute."

"Yes, my child; and it is a beautiful story, and you told it so nicely. It is very interesting and you must tell me another to-morrow. But now, dear, you must really go to bed, because I am going to bed, too. That man startled me so," she said, passing her small white hand over her pale forehead and then staring into the fire.

"Well, I don't wonder," answered Nellie in a patronising tone. "Such a dreadful night too! Of course, it would startle anybody. But he won't try again, and you can scold Mary to-morrow and then she can scold her young man."

The child spoke so naturally that all doubts vanished from Mrs. Goddard's mind. She refleted that children are much more apt to see things as they are, than grown people whose nerves are out of order. Nellie's conclusions were perfectly logical, and it seemed folly to doubt them. She determined that Mary should certainly be scolded on the morrow and she unconsciously resolved in her mind the words she should use; for she was rather a timid woman and stood a little in awe of her stalwart Berkshire cook, with her mighty arms and her red face, and her uncommonly plain language.

"Yes dear," she said more quietly than she had been able to speak for some time, "I have no doubt you are quite right.   I thought I heard his footsteps just now, going down the path.   So he will not trouble us any more to-night.   And now darling, kneel down and say your prayers, and then we will go to bed."

So Nellie, reassured by the news that her mother was going to bed, too, knelt down as she had done every night during the eleven years of her life, and clasped her hands together, beneath her mother's.   Then she cleared her throat, then she glanced at the clock, then she looked for one moment into the sweet serious violet eyes that looked down on her so lovingly, and then at last she bent her lovely little head and began to say her prayers, there, by the fire, at her mother's knees, while angry storm howled fiercely without and shook the closed panes and shutters and occasional drops of rain, falling down the short chimney, sputtered in the smouldering coal fire.

"Our Father which art in Heaven, Hallowed be Thy Name, Thy Kingdom come——"

Nellie gave a loud scream and springing up from her knees flung her arms around her mother's neck, in uttermost, wildest terror.

"Mamma, mamma!" she cried looking, and yet hardly daring to look, back towards the closed window. "It called 'MARY GODDARD'! It is you, mamma! Oh!"

There was no mistaking it this time. While Nellie was saying her prayer there had come three sharp and distinct raps upon the wooden shutter, and a voice, not loud but clear, penetrating into the room in spite of wind and storm and rain.

"Mary Goddard! Mary Goddard!" it said.

Mrs. Goddard started to her feet, lifting Nellie bodily from the ground in her agony of terror; staring round the room wildly as though in search of some possible escape.

"I must come in! I will come in!" said the voice again.

"Oh don't let him in! Mamma! Don't let

him in!" moaned the terrified child upon her breast, clinging to her and weighing her down, and grasping her neck and arm with convulsive strength.

But in moments of great agitation timid people, or people who are thought timid, not uncommonly do brave things.   Mrs. Goddard unclasped Nellie's hold and forced the terror-struck child into a deep chair.

"Stay there, darling," she said with unnatural calmness.   "Do not be afraid.   I will go and open the door."

Nellie was now too much frightened to resist. Mrs. Goddard went out into the little passage which was dimly lighted by a hanging lamp, and closed the door of the drawing-room behind her. She could hear Nellie's occasional convulsive sobs distinctly.   For one moment she paused, her right hand on the lock of the front door, her left hand pressed to her side, leaning against the wall of the passage.   Then she turned the key and the handle and drew the door in towards her.   A violent gust of wind, full of cold and drenching rain, whirled into the passage and almost blinded her.   The lamp flickered in the lantern overhead. But she looked boldly out, facing the wind and weather.

"Come in!" she called in a low voice.

Immediately there was a sound as of footsteps coming from the direction of the drawing-room window, across the wet slate flags which surrounded the cottage, and a moment afterwards, peering through the darkness, Mrs. Goddard saw a man with a ghastly face standing before her in the rain.

END OF VOL. I.